DANNY ORLIS
AND THE
DRY GULCH MYSTERY

DANNY ORLIS

AND THE

DRY GULCH MYSTERY

BERNARD PALMER

Please note that several books in the Danny Orlis series are published by Sword of the Lord Publications and are available for purchase on their website, www.swordbooks.com.

Aneko Press *Youth*

www.anekopress.com

Aneko Press, Life Sentence Publishing, and our logos are trademarks of Life Sentence Publishing, Inc.
203 E. Birch Street
P.O. Box 652
Abbotsford, WI 54405

JUVENILE FICTION / Religious / Christian / Action & Adventure

Paperback ISBN: 979-8-88936-052-0
eBook ISBN: 979-8-88936-053-7

10 9 8 7 6 5 4 3 2 1

Available where books are sold

CONTENTS

CHAPTER 1

TEXAS AGAIN

Clarence and Carmen Roper sent three airline tickets to the triplets, and Danny and Kay took them to Minneapolis where they boarded a flight to Texas. Although the boys and DeeDee had not been too excited about making the trip when Danny first let them read the letter from their mother's sister, their excitement grew as they neared the airport where they were to land.

"Do you suppose Uncle Clarence still has those saddle horses he let us ride when we were here last year?" Del asked.

"If he doesn't," Doug replied, "he'll have some others."

"I don't want another one. I'd like to have the one I had before."

DeeDee, who was seated nearest the window, peered out.

"I sure hope they'll be there to meet us."

When neither of the boys spoke, she continued.

"What do you suppose it'll be like at the ranch now that Aunt Carmen is a Christian?"

Del ran his hand through his closely cropped hair.

"If it has the same effect on Uncle Clarence that it had when Phil made his decision for Christ, I'm not sure I even want to be around," he answered. "He can scare the life out of a guy without half trying."

"He must have changed his mind a little or he wouldn't even have us on the ranch," Doug reminded him. "You know what he said when he found out. He blamed us, and I thought we were all going to get skinned alive."

The warning to fasten seat belts flashed on.

The entire Roper family was waiting for them in the terminal building. Aunt Carmen swept them into her arms, talking a mixture of English and Spanish at the same time as she was laughing and crying. Phil, Marie, and the triplets were all talking at once while Uncle Clarence stood to one side, watching with obvious amusement. It was two or three minutes before he spoke.

"Well, if you think you're all through talking and crying," he said, "maybe we'd better head for the car. We've got quite a drive ahead of us, and I'd like to get back to the ranch before dark if we can."

On the way to the car, Del turned to their uncle

and asked the question that had been bothering him ever since they decided to visit the ranch.

"Uncle Clarence," he began uncertainly, "do you still have the horses we rode when we were here before?"

"We've got a lot of horses on the ranch," Clarence replied evasively.

"But do you still have the ones that we rode? That's what I want to know."

"Yep, we've still got 'em," he said, laughing pleasantly. He unlocked the car and put their suitcases in the back. "As a matter of fact, when we got word that you were coming, I had one of the hands catch 'em up and ride 'em for a while so they wouldn't be quite so salty."

Del beamed. "That's great!"

When they got back to the Circle R, Phil took the boys down to the barn to look at the horses. They were the same as they had been when the triplets left almost a year before. Doug eyed them approvingly.

"It's sure going to be fun to do some riding again."

"You can say that again," Del added.

They helped Phil throw down some hay for the horses and got some oats out of the bin for them.

"Do you suppose we can go riding tomorrow morning?" Del asked.

"I sure hope so. I've got something I want you to help me with." There was mystery in Phil's tone. "It's this way–"

DeeDee and Marie came into the barn just then, and Phil stopped in the middle of a sentence.

DeeDee rushed up to the horse she had ridden the summer before.

"Oh, there you are, Lady." She turned to Marie. "Isn't she beautiful?"

"I guess she's all right."

"I think she's the most beautiful horse I've ever seen."

Del and Doug glanced at their sister with ill-concealed disgust.

"Aren't there some dishes you ought to be doing, DeeDee?"

"Do the dishes?" she echoed. "We haven't even eaten yet."

"What about helping make the beds?"

She eyed Doug suspiciously. "What's the matter? Why is it that you don't want us around?"

He laughed uneasily. "What makes you think we don't want you around?"

Marie took DeeDee by the arm. "Come on. We don't want to stay out here anyway."

When they were gone, Doug and Del turned eagerly back to their cousin.

"Now, what were you saying, Phil?"

Phil lowered his voice to a whisper.

"There's something mysterious going on here – right on the ranch!"

Their eyes widened.

Phil was about to continue but before he could do so they heard a footstep outside the barn. He clamped his mouth tightly and warned them to silence with his eyes. Fear tingled icily up and down their spines.

Doug drew a long, deep breath. Their stay at the Circle R was going to be an exciting one. The mystery Phil was talking about had to be something important. He couldn't fake the excited gleam in his eyes or the fear that edged his thin voice.

And whatever it was, he didn't want anyone else to know about it. That made it even more exciting and mysterious.

"Let's get up early in the morning," Phil said loudly enough for anyone outside to hear, "and go for that ride you guys have been talking so much about."

At that instant Uncle Clarence thrust his head in the barn door.

"Mom sent me out to get you guys," he said. "Dinner'll be ready by the time you get to the house and get washed."

Doug eyed their uncle quizzically as they sat up to the table in the big ranch kitchen. The last time they were here he got all worked up because they had asked the blessing before they ate. Doug wondered what was going to happen this time.

He did not have to wait long. Clarence's glance swept the table.

"Should we have DeeDee give thanks for the food before we eat?"

DeeDee's head jerked up, her eyes widening.

Clarence grinned. "What's the matter, DeeDee?" he asked. "Did I surprise you?"

She nodded.

"Now, don't think I've got that religion of yours," Clarence said firmly. "I just made a little deal with your Aunt Carmen, that's all."

Thankfully DeeDee bowed her head and prayed.

Doug and Del wanted to get Phil aside as soon as they finished eating and find out what he had been talking about in the barn, but there was no chance for that. Uncle Clarence went into the living room with them and had the boys sit down.

"I want to hear all about that ranch you're living on up in Minnesota before Carmen and the girls come in. They talk so fast and furious I never would be able to find out anything."

"Well, in the first place, it's not a ranch." Del spoke slowly. "I guess you couldn't even say that it's a farm. Danny doesn't do any farming. We just live in the country."

"But it's great," Doug put in. "Danny says we can get a cow and some pigs and chickens this fall if we'll take care of them. That way we can earn some money for college."

The rancher nodded his approval. "Sounds like a good idea. That way you won't have to ask anyone for a lot of help. Every boy your age ought to have something to do."

Clarence continued to ply them with questions and, with gentle insistence, got the information he wanted. How did they like working on a place in the country? Were Danny and Kay good to them? Did they have everything they needed? Did they have to stay home from school to work?

When Carmen and the girls came in, he directed his attention to DeeDee. What did she think of Danny and Kay Orlis?

DeeDee's face lit up. "Oh, they're wonderful!"

Her uncle scowled. "Oh, come now," he exclaimed, "they're not as good as all that."

"But they are. They're just great." Her expression changed, as though she suddenly realized that what she had said might sound disloyal. "Of course, it isn't like living with Mom and Dad, but they do try to get everything we need and help us to live good Christian lives."

Carmen smiled graciously. "I'm sure they're very fine parents," she said. "And I don't have any doubts that you're being raised exactly the way your mom and dad would have wanted you to be raised."

Clarence fingered the cigarette in his hand. Once or twice he acted as though he wanted to say more, but he did not. He was quiet the rest of the evening, in spite of the fact that nobody mentioned Danny and Kay or spiritual things again.

The triplets had many questions. They asked about the friends they had made at the ranch when they were there before, about the work that needed doing, and a hundred other things. Questions tumbled out until everyone was laughing and talking at once.

At last Clarence glanced at his watch and got quickly to his feet.

"It's after ten o'clock," he exclaimed. "I didn't realize it was so late. I'm going in and listen to the rest of the news and then go to bed. We've got to roll out mighty early in the morning."

"You aren't going to insist that the boys get up early, are you, Clarence?" Carmen asked. "After all, they just got here."

"Oh, we want to get up early in the morning," Del said.

"That's right," Doug added. "I mean – you don't know how long we've been looking forward to getting back here and–"

Both Clarence and Carmen stared at him, questions glinting in their eyes.

"What do you mean?" the rancher demanded.

Doug looked at them blankly, realizing that what he had said sounded different than he wanted it to sound.

"Nothing–nothing at all." He swallowed hard. "I just mean we've been lonesome for you all."

"And for the ranch," Del said, "and–and the horses."

Their uncle's face grew stern. "Now, I want you to tell me the truth," he blurted. "Are you happy with that Orlis guy and his wife?"

"Sure we are. Why?"

"Are they mean to you?"

"They couldn't be mean if they tried," Del told him. "Of course, they make us mind, but we can't say they've ever been mean to us."

Roper still was not satisfied. He stopped questioning the boys and directed his attention to their sister.

"Is that the truth, DeeDee? Has either of them ever struck you or the boys?"

DeeDee paused. "I don't think they have." She wrinkled her nose thoughtfully. "Danny did swat Del on the seat a couple of times for fighting with Doug, but that's the only time I can think of."

Del broke in. "But it didn't hurt any. I hardly felt it."

"The only times we've been punished have been when we deserved it," Doug explained.

Roper seemed disappointed. "It's a good thing for them that they've treated you okay," he went on. "That's all I can say. If they'd been mean to you, you'd be staying right here on the ranch with us. This is where you belong anyway."

The triplets didn't understand what he meant, but they didn't feel free to ask him to explain. They said good night and started to their rooms, but Aunt Carmen stopped them.

"There are too many of us to have devotions in the bedroom tonight," she said. "Why don't we have them out here?"

Clarence got up and left the room quickly.

Ignoring his dad's actions, Phil got the Bible and took it to his mother.

"We'll continue to read from the book of Acts," she said.

It was easy for the triplets to see that she had become familiar with the Bible. She pronounced the names easily and read in a way that made the story live. When she finished reading, she asked for prayer requests much the way Danny and Kay did, and she had Del and DeeDee lead in prayer.

Phil was the last to enter the bedroom he was sharing with his two cousins in their stay on the ranch.

"Well?"

Both Doug and Del knew what he meant. He was wondering what they thought of their Aunt Carmen now that she had made a decision for Christ.

"It sure is different around here since your mom became a Christian, isn't it?"

"You can say that again. You wouldn't even know this was the same house. Mom reads the Bible and prays and everything."

Del sat down and loosened his shoelaces.

"What does your dad think about it?"

Phil sat down across from the boys. "I thought he'd really blow a fuse when it happened," he began. "You know what he did when I told him I was a Christian. I guess he did get awful mad for a while, but when he saw the change in Mom's life, it made him see that being a Christian wasn't so bad after all."

They got ready for bed and Phil switched off the light. "I'll see you guys in the morning."

Doug sat up quickly. "Hey! Wait a minute! I just thought of something! What about that mystery you were going to tell us about?"

There was a brief silence. Then Phil spoke in a low voice. "Well, you remember that old house in the dry gulch that cuts across our west pasture?"

"You mean the one we went to the night Marie got thrown and that bad storm came up?"

"That's the one." Phil cleared his throat. "There are some strange things going on over there."

Doug and Del gasped.

"I don't know what it is for sure," Phil went on in a hoarse whisper, "but there are lights in the house at night."

"When did you see this?" Del asked excitedly.

"I haven't seen it for myself, but I heard one of the hands talking about it a couple of days ago. He was chasing strays in that part of the prairie after dark. When he saw a light in the old house, he got curious and rode over to see what was going on, but as he rode up the light went out."

"Did he go inside?"

"He started to but got scared. And when he got back to the ranch, he couldn't get anyone to ride over there with him. They all laughed and accused him of seeing things."

"Didn't anyone ever go back over there?" Doug asked.

"He told Dad and the foreman about it, and they were just like the other men. They razzed him so much he wouldn't go back," Phil replied.

There was a long silence.

"Didn't they believe him?" Del asked.

"This guy is always pulling some kind of joke," Phil said, "so Dad thinks he's just trying to kid us."

Doug grunted. "What kind of joke is *that?*"

Phil lowered his voice to a whisper. "That's exactly what I thought. I was going to go over there and take a look myself. I even started that direction the other afternoon, but when I got close to the arroyo–" His voice choked off.

"You saw the lights yourself?" There was awe in Del's voice.

"No, but I thought I saw someone hiding in the brush!"

CHAPTER 2

STRANGE TRACKS

That night Doug dreamed of lights in old, abandoned houses and strange dark shadows that lurked ominously behind every bush. Once or twice he awoke suddenly, sure that he was about to be grabbed and carried off into the mesquite.

He sat up for a moment, looking over at Phil and Del who were sleeping peacefully. His temper flared. What was the matter with them anyway? Didn't they know those mysterious lights and shadows could mean almost anything? He lay back once more and tried to sleep, but every time he closed his eyes, those dreadful lights came back.

Doug had been to the old building on the lip of the arroyo only once, almost a year ago, but every detail was etched sharply in his mind. He could see the weathered siding, the sagging door, the broken windows. He could almost hear the wind sighing eerily through the empty rooms. Doug didn't think he slept at all, but when morning came Del and Phil had to shake him roughly to waken him.

"Doug!" Del cried. "Come on! Pile out! Are you going to sleep all day?"

He jerked awake. His first wild thought was that the shadows of his dream had come to life and were carrying him off again. "Hey!" His voice was hoarse. "What's going on here?"

He jumped out of bed and looked around, sleep keeping his eyes from focusing properly.

"Nothing's going on, except that you're acting like a wild man," Phil said, laughing. "It's morning – time to get up."

"Yeah. We've got to help Uncle Clarence today. Remember?"

Wide awake at last, Doug grinned sheepishly. "You guys should've been with me last night in my dream," he told them. "You don't know what I've been through!"

"Whatever it was, it must've been bad."

"It was. Let me tell you."

They dressed hurriedly and went down for breakfast. Although Clarence had talked as though he wanted to start work early that morning, he changed his mind for some reason. He left the table without giving them any instructions and started outdoors. Phil called after him. "Hey, Dad, what did you have lined up for us to do this morning?"

The rancher stopped and pivoted to face them. "Well, I'll tell you." His broad grin flashed. "Why don't you go out and have some fun for a few days? Ride those horses and take a good look around the ranch."

"But I thought you said you had some things you wanted us to do?" Phil said.

His dad frowned. "What's the matter? Can't a guy change his mind if he wants to?"

"Oh, sure. Sure." Phil turned to his cousins. "Come on, before he changes his mind again."

Clarence laughed good-naturedly. "Now, that's what I call a good piece of advice."

The boys hurried out and saddled their horses.

Phil said, "This is a break. Now we're going to be able to go down to that old house the first thing."

Doug felt the color leave his cheeks. "I don't know whether that's such a break or not," he said. "If you'd been along in my dream last night–"

Del glanced toward the ranch house.

"We'd better hurry or the girls will have the dishes done and we'll have to take them along."

The boys rode out through the gate that led to the west pasture and across the bleak, mesquite-dotted prairie. Doug glanced about uneasily.

"You know," he said, "it sure would be simple for somebody to jump us here if they wanted to."

Del's eyes widened. "What gave you that happy thought?"

"I was just thinking about the things Phil told us: the mysterious lights and the man hiding in the brush. If anybody did want to get us, this'd be the best place I know of."

"Well, quit thinking about it or you'll have us all so jumpy we'll want to turn around and go back."

"Maybe that would be a good idea, at that," Doug observed.

Phil broke in. "If you guys want to turn around, it's all right with me," he said. "I just thought you'd like to get in on tracing this thing down." He reined to a stop as he spoke and looked from one to another.

"Oh, no," Doug answered. "I don't think much of the idea of going over there, but I don't think I'd sleep nights if we didn't find out for sure what's going on." He laughed nervously. "You can't pay any attention to what I say. I just get jumpy once in a while."

"How about you, Del?" his cousin asked.

"I'm with you all the way."

They rode on, picking their way slowly among the cactus and scrawny, crooked mesquite that looked half dead but stubbornly kept on growing. They crossed a narrow gulch and angled south until they came to a muddy little stream.

"It sure would be hard to herd cattle in here," Del said.

Phil nodded. "You can say that again. We'll be putting a herd in here in a few days, so you'll get a taste of it before long. You go chasing cattle in this stuff and you soon see why most of the hands wear leather chaps."

"You mean there aren't any cattle in here now?" Doug asked.

"Nope. Dad's still got 'em on the winter pasture. He was telling me the other day that he's going to send someone down here to take a look at the grass, and if it looks okay, he plans on moving some cattle in before long."

Del frowned. "He already checked the pasture, didn't he?"

Phil shook his head. "Not that I know of," he said. "Why?"

"I've been seeing horse tracks along the creek, and when you said that somebody was going to check the range, I figured that was the one who'd made them," Del answered.

Phil's face blanched. "Where have you seen tracks?" In spite of himself his voice tightened.

"All along here." In a moment or two Del reined up and pointed. "There's some now."

Phil swung off his horse and knelt beside the tracks, studying them intently.

"What is it?" Doug asked.

He did not reply. Del and Doug dismounted and hunkered down beside him. "What's so interesting about those tracks?" Del inquired.

It was a long minute before Phil spoke. "These

tracks weren't made by a Circle R cow pony. I can tell you that."

"How do you know?" asked Doug.

"Dad doesn't use shoes shaped like these. The ones we get come from a place in Brownsville. They're narrower than these and come back further here." He pointed to the open end of the shoes.

"Are you sure?" inquired Del.

"Sure, I'm sure. I've helped shoe too many of our horses not to know what our shoes look like."

There was silence. Then Del asked, "Who do you suppose it is?"

Phil shook his head. "I don't know, but these tracks are headed straight for that abandoned old house!"

For the space of a minute or two the boys stared at the tracks.

"What do you think, Phil?" Doug asked. "Should we follow them?"

Phil squatted down beside the tracks and traced the nearest with his forefinger. It was a while before he spoke.

"I'd sure like to know where the guy who rode this horse came from," he muttered, "and what he's doing on our ranch."

"We could follow these tracks for a little way," Del suggested. "At least to find out for sure where they're going."

Phil squinted up at the sun. "We'd better be getting back before mom and dad start worrying about us," he said. "We didn't tell them how long we'd be gone. Besides, I'm starved."

"Me too," Doug put in.

"We can come back again tomorrow and follow these tracks," Phil said.

Del was reluctant to give up even for a day, but there was no choice. He joined Doug and Phil as they mounted their horses.

"Do you think there'd be any chance of–of getting your dad to come along with us tomorrow?" Doug asked.

Phil shook his head. "The way Dad made fun of that cowhand who told him about the light in the old house, I don't think we've got a chance of getting him to go with us," he explained. "He'd say we've been reading too many mystery stories."

They turned back toward the ranch buildings. Every now and then Phil glanced over his shoulder, still wondering about the strange tracks. The same subject was on Del's mind, too. He kept trying to figure out who could have made the tracks and what he had been doing on the Roper ranch.

Clarence was in the barn currying his saddle horse when he heard the boys ride up. "Hi, guys," he called out. "I didn't think you'd be back quite so soon."

The boys dismounted slowly.

"Neither did we," Phil answered.

"Don't tell me that you boys have been seeing strange lights out in the summer pasture, too."

"Aw, Dad!" Phil's voice raised in protest. "How could we see any lights in the daytime?"

Clarence chuckled. "I figured it wouldn't be quite so scary seeing mysterious lights in the daytime. If I was going to see anything like that, I believe I'd choose daylight every time."

Phil glanced helplessly at his companions. Now they would know that it wouldn't do any good to talk to his dad about going with them. He already had his mind made up about things like that. But Phil had to talk to him anyway. At least he had to tell him about the strange tracks.

"Dad, we saw some tracks out in the pasture that weren't made by one of our horses."

The smile faded from Clarence's lips, but his eyes were twinkling. "Don't tell me. Let me guess. They were elephant tracks."

Phil frowned in frustration. "Aw, Dad! You know the kind of tracks we're talking about. We saw the tracks of a strange horse along the creek."

"Did you now?" Clarence countered.

"If you don't believe it, we'll take you out and show you."

Clarence's smile returned. "If I want to look at horse tracks, I can find some a whole lot closer to home than that."

Phil turned to his companions. "See?" he said. "What'd I tell you? Dad doesn't believe there are any strange tracks or lights."

Before either of the boys could speak, Clarence went on. "Oh, I believe somebody's been seeing something out there, all right," he told them. "I think the moon was shining on the window of that old house when our nervous cowboy went by it a week or so ago. And I think you boys must have seen the tracks of our own cow ponies. That's what I think." He laughed heartily.

Phil turned away. "Come on, guys. We'll have to work this out by ourselves."

* * *

The day after the Davis boys and Phil had seen the strange tracks, Clarence had them move a small herd of yearlings from one pasture to the other after checking the creek to be sure there was plenty of water for them. It was almost suppertime when they rode back.

"I sure hope Dad doesn't have anything for us to do tomorrow," Phil said. "I want to go back and follow those tracks far enough to see where they go–"

Doug squirmed uncomfortably in his saddle. "Do you mean that?"

Phil leaned forward and spoke in a whisper. "You aren't backing out on me, are you?"

"Who, me?" Doug forced a thin laugh. "I'm as game as you and Del are – I think."

Clarence came up just then, and the boys changed the subject quickly.

That night the Roper family and the Davis triplets were still at the dinner table when the ranch foreman came in. Clarence got to his feet, concern tightening the muscles in his face. His foreman seldom came to the ranch house, especially not at mealtime. Conversation ceased.

"What's on your mind?" Clarence asked.

The foreman shifted from one foot to the other. "I hate to bother you like this, Clarence, but I've got something here that I think you ought to see."

The rancher scowled. "Can't it wait?"

"I suppose it could," the foreman replied. "But if I were in your place, I think I'd want to know about it right away."

CHAPTER 3

THE SHEEP HIDE

Clarence followed his foreman to the door. "What's up?" he asked. Although they had gone out on the porch, he spoke so loudly those at the table could hear.

"You know some of the boys have been talkin' about strange things goin' on around here?"

"You don't put any faith in those stories, do you?" Clarence queried.

"Maybe not. But I think there's some truth to this one. Somebody's rustlin' stock. Take a quick look at this."

Phil left the table and went quickly to the kitchen door. Doug and Del glanced at their aunt questioningly. They didn't want to leave the table without her permission, but they both were so curious they could scarcely sit still. She smiled faintly and nodded. They joined Phil at the door.

The foreman was standing on the bottom step holding out a small, woolly hide.

"We found this hide in the north pasture this afternoon. Somebody killed him and skinned him out."

Clarence stared. "That's the hide of a lamb!"

"I didn't say it wasn't! But it was rustled. That's the main thing."

"But we don't run any sheep," Clarence said, "so I don't see how this concerns us."

"We don't run any sheep," Ed replied. "But as far as I'm concerned, anybody who'd steal a lamb would steal cattle if they got the chance. So I think we ought to do something about it."

Clarence's lips tightened. "You might be right about that. What do you figure on doing about it?"

"Don't know yet," the foreman retorted. "I ain't figgered that out. But right now I thought you ought to know about it."

"Thanks, Ed. I appreciate that." Clarence examined the hide with an experienced eye. "That must be one of McAllister's sheep. I'll drive over there tomorrow and tell him about it so he can keep his eyes open."

When the foreman was gone, Phil looked up into his dad's clear, blue eyes.

"What do you think about the strange tracks we saw in the north pasture now, Dad?" he said.

"It was probably some cowboy riding through who decided he wanted some fresh meat."

But the boy still wasn't satisfied. It didn't add up

to him. "Did you ever hear of a cowboy who'd kill a sheep and eat it?"

Clarence ran his calloused fingers through his hair. "Nope. Can't say that I have."

They went back to the table and finished eating, but Clarence only toyed with his food. He remained at the table after the others had finished eating and had excused themselves.

DeeDee began to clear the table. "Marie," she said, "you washed the dishes this noon. I'll do them tonight."

Carmen spoke up. "I'll wash the dishes tonight, DeeDee."

"Oh, no, Aunt Carmen. Marie and I will take care of them. Won't we, Marie?"

Reluctantly Marie nodded.

Clarence got to his feet suddenly and touched his wife's arm. "Come on, Carmen. The girls say they'll finish the dishes. Let 'em."

"But–"

"I've just been thinking. I'd better go over and tell McAllister about his sheep tonight. I'd like to have you ride with me."

Carmen got ready quickly, and they drove over to the neighboring ranch.

The following morning Phil and the Davis boys left the ranch house soon after breakfast. They hurried down to the barn, saddled their horses, and started across the yard to the narrow road that led to the highway.

Del glanced over his shoulder. "Are they coming?" he asked.

Phil shook his head. "If our luck holds, we'll be able to get away without those girls again."

Doug spoke up. "I don't think we've got a chance. Did you see how they were watching us at breakfast? They know we're up to something and they're going to get in on it if they possibly can."

Del groaned. "You're right. Here they come."

DeeDee and Marie came running from the ranch house, yelling, and waving at them.

"Where are you going?" they cried.

"For a ride." Del made no attempt to hide his disgust.

DeeDee looked past her brothers at Phil. "Can we go along?"

Del and Doug stared hard at Phil, shaking their heads, but he acted as though he didn't even see them. He shrugged his shoulders indifferently. "Doesn't make any difference to me."

With that DeeDee turned to Marie. "See, what did I tell you? I knew Phil would take us along if we asked him." She glanced significantly at her brothers. "He's not like some other people I know."

"He's never been that way when I ask him to let me go with him," Marie said. "He always says I can't go."

"He must be gettin' soft or something," Doug muttered under his breath.

The boys went back to the barn and helped the girls saddle their horses. Although they hurried as fast as they could, it cost them half an hour's time. Even Phil was grumbling by the time they were ready.

DeeDee turned to Phil. "Where are we going?"

"For a ride," he said mysteriously.

"But where?" Her gaze met his insistently. "And what are we going to do?"

"For now, we're just going to ride," he answered shortly.

"And if you don't want to do that," Del said, "you could stay home. It'll be all right with us."

For answer she stuck her tongue out at him and made a little face.

DeeDee saw that she was not going to get any more information from any of them and fell silent. Phil led the little party across the pasture to the place where they had first seen the strange tracks. At last he reined to a halt.

"Here we are," he said. He swung off his horse and squatted beside the trail to examine the tracks once more. They were hard now, yet the distinctive characteristics were still discernible. "Yep," he said, "it's them, all right."

Del nodded. "Now to see where they go." Marie and DeeDee stared, eyes widening.

"Is–is this what you came out to do?" Marie asked, her voice quavering uneasily.

"That's right. We're going to follow those tracks."

"Who do you suppose made them? The man who killed the lamb?" Marie asked.

Phil scowled and traced the outline of the horseshoe with his finger. "Maybe," he said, "and maybe not. That's one of the things we've got to find out." He turned back to his sister. "What're you going to do now? Are you going to stay with us, or do you plan on turning around and going home?"

Marie glanced down the pasture in the direction of the ranch house and then looked at DeeDee.

"I–I think we're going to stay with you," she said after some hesitation.

"Okay. Only remember, you had your chance to go back, and you turned it down."

Marie's cheeks paled. "Do–do you think it's dangerous?"

"It could be." Phil lowered his voice to a whisper. "It could be mighty dangerous!"

The color fled from DeeDee's cheeks, and her gaze shifted from Phil to her brothers and back again. "You–you're just trying to scare us," she said hopefully. "Aren't you, Phil?"

There was no answer.

"Aren't you?"

Still her cousin did not reply. At last in desperation she turned to Del.

"Isn't he trying to scare us?"

There was a brief pause.

"Well–" The words came out with some reluctance. "We don't know who made these tracks."

At that Phil spoke up. "That's right, DeeDee. We don't know who made the tracks, but we're not going to follow them far enough to get into any trouble. I can tell you that right now."

"Are you sure?"

"That's a promise," he continued. "We'll follow them far enough to see whether they lead to the old house or not. That's all we've been planning on doing."

DeeDee sighed in relief.

Interest glittered in Marie's somber black eyes. "You know," she said in a hushed voice, "I've been wondering if these tracks could have anything to do with the strange lights in the old house."

"So have we," her brother retorted, impatient to be on the way. "But I can tell you this much. We're not going to find out a thing until we get a move on and get down to the pasture."

With that he nicked his mount lightly in the ribs with his heels and the wiry pony broke into a brisk trot. The others fell in behind him in single file. Excitement overcame Marie's fear and she glanced from one side to the other with growing anticipation.

* * *

Clarence had planned to ride that morning, but he got sidetracked into working around the buildings. He repaired the rigging on a couple of saddles and then went into the house and worked on the books. Shortly after ten o'clock Carmen came into the office with a pot of coffee and some cookies.

"It's time to take a little break," she said brightly.

"It's not hard to get me to take a break when I've had to mess with figures. I'd rather be out on the range riding herd any day."

"I know." She passed him the cookies. "I didn't think you'd mind if I came in and disturbed you."

"You know I never mind when you come in, Carmen," he told her.

He had to admit that since she decided to be a Christian or whatever she called it, things were different around the house. Her always volatile temper was strangely tamed, and she was so much more considerate of him and the kids and everyone else than she had been before.

"I've been thinking about that sheep hide," she began, "and the strange light in the old house and those tracks the boys found. Do you suppose anyone is actually living out there, Clarence?"

"I doubt it," he said, as though shrugging her doubts aside. "If anyone was living in the old house, he wouldn't be foolish enough to kill a sheep and not bury the hide. He'd know we would start looking around right away." He sipped his coffee. "That hide would be a dead giveaway. The thing that really bothers me about this is that hide being out where it could be found. I can't imagine anyone smart enough to steal a critter – even a sheep – being so stupid."

"Maybe you're right." Carmen spoke thoughtfully. "But I can't help worrying a bit about the kids. I wish they hadn't ridden off in the west pasture until we find out for sure what's going on."

Clarence chuckled good-naturedly. "Now, quit fussing about them like an old mother hen, Carmen. They're all right, and they're going to be all right. They'll come riding back here about four o'clock this afternoon, hungry as starving coyotes and so tired they won't want to do anything but fall into bed."

"I should have fixed lunch for them."

He reached over and patted her reassuringly on the arm. "There you go again. Will you quit fussing about those young ones? It's not going to hurt them to get a little hungry."

Carmen poured another cup of coffee for her husband and sat down across from him again.

"I'm not as upset as I sound."

"That's a good thing." His laughter reverberated through the paneled room. "You sound right now as though you'd like to call out a platoon of Texas Rangers to hunt them out and see that they get something to eat and have their boots on in case it rains."

After a moment she changed the subject. "It's good to have the triplets here, isn't it?"

He nodded thoughtfully. "It's strange, Carmen, but I've been thinking about the same thing all morning. I didn't realize how much I thought of them – how much we all think of them – until they came back this summer. I'm sorry that I made you get them out of the house. Somebody should have slugged me."

Carmen set her cup on the edge of his desk. It would have been easy for her to have lashed out at him, to have reminded him of how she had pleaded with him to let Rosalita's children stay on the ranch, and how he had raged at her in return. But she did not do so. Instead she voiced something else that had been increasingly on her mind of late.

"I've been thinking that it would be so good to have them living with us again," Carmen said. "They're such a good influence on Philip and Marie."

"I've noticed that," Clarence acknowledged.

"That's because they're Christians."

She hadn't planned on saying what she did. It slipped out. Realizing what she had said, she glanced quickly up at Clarence.

"I wouldn't know about that." An edge came into his voice that she hadn't heard for weeks.

There was a long, pained silence. Then Carmen said, "It seems to me that they're a whole lot more agreeable now than they were when they stayed with us last fall."

Picking up his coffee, Clarence went to the window where he stood staring across the grasslands. "I think they're more used to us now and we're more used to them. I don't think it's that crazy, mixed-up religion of theirs."

"You might be right that we've had a chance to get better acquainted," Carmen said, "but that's not the only thing that is making them such a good influence on Philip and Marie. I know from the impact their lives had on mine that it's their faith that makes the difference."

He turned the matter over in his mind, examining it from every side. "But they were religious all the time," he countered. "If that's what's made the difference, why would it show up now?"

"I've been thinking about that. They were still upset about their parents' death when they were here before. And they didn't know us very well either." She paused. "And what they did know of us wasn't very pleasant."

Clarence bristled. "What do you mean by that crack?"

"I'm sorry. I was just thinking about the way we treated them and Rosalita and Jerry when they came to visit." She smiled. "You'll have to admit that neither of us treated the family very well."

"I guess you've got a point there."

"And now," Carmen went on, "we're getting to see them when they're not under tension and when we can see what they're really like."

Clarence came back and sat down again. "I've been

trying to make up my mind whether to ask you this or not, Carmen," he said. "If you would like to have me do it, I'll try to get them back legally."

Her gaze met his. "But we signed papers giving the triplets to Danny and Kay Orlis."

"There might be something we can do about it," her husband continued. "I've got some slick lawyers. They just might be able to figure out something that would get them back for us, for a price."

His dark-haired wife eyed him, a new longing in her face. "It would be wonderful to have Rosalita's children as our own," she said. "I don't know of anything that would make me happier."

"Then it's settled. I'll go into town tomorrow morning and get the lawyers started on it. They might be able to wind things up in a month, so the kids won't even have to go back north."

But Carmen shook her head. "We can't go back on our word," she said. "We told the Orlises they could have them."

At last Clarence spoke. "We gave our word – at least you told them they could have the kids," he said. "But just suppose there was fraud involved. What then?"

Her eyes crinkled questioningly. "What do you mean?"

"Suppose there was something that we didn't understand about the deal," he said. "Suppose they hadn't represented things as they really are."

Disapproval darkened Carmen's gaze. "We couldn't say anything like that, Clarence. It wouldn't be true. They would prove it in court."

He laughed shortly. "If they do, we'll carry it up. I got to thinking about this last night. Danny and Kay Orlis are just poor missionaries. They haven't got the money to take a case to court and keep fighting it. They'll have to give up."

Carmen shook her head. "It wouldn't be honest to do anything like that. As badly as I'd like to have DeeDee and the boys, I don't want to get them that way."

Clarence nodded. The old needling came back to his voice. "That's right. I'd almost forgotten you got bit by the same religious bug that ruined Rosalita's life. So we'll think of some other way to get them."

She did not answer him.

"I think my attorney could come up with something else that would make an even stronger case. You know, Carmen, most of these laws have some sort of loophole that a smart attorney can squirm through. What if it did cost us a few thousand dollars or so? If we get custody of the triplets again, I think it would be worth it."

Carmen was a long while in replying, but not because of indecision. "I don't care what method we would try, Clarence," she told him, her voice clear and firm. "And I don't care whether it would be successful or not. I don't want to do it. And besides, I don't believe our laws were made so that someone can run roughshod over someone else just because he has more money."

"Well," he said, "we could try."

"No," she said, "we aren't going to try to get the triplets back. We asked Danny and Kay to take them, and they agreed to do it when we said they could legally adopt them. It almost breaks my heart to know that Rosalita's children belong to someone else, but we're not going against our word."

"Not even to get the triplets back?" he asked.

"Not even to get them back."

The clock in the living room struck the hour. He remained motionless until all was silent once more.

"I never thought I'd live long enough to hear you say a thing like that."

CHAPTER 4

LEFTY

Phil had no difficulty following the trail left by the peculiar horseshoes, even though it was several days old. There were some things about the tracks that bothered him. The rider, whoever he was, had not been concerned about hiding his tracks. He either didn't think he had to worry about anyone following him – or he wanted to make it appear as though he had nothing to hide.

Maybe that was it, Phil reasoned to himself as they rode along. The stranger had ridden out in the open as boldly as one of the cowhands hunting maverick steers. He might figure that would make it easier for him to convince anyone who stumbled onto him that he had a right to be there or that he didn't plan any mischief.

In spite of himself, Phil's pulse hammered at a faster pace. The rider was not going to get away with that, as far as he was concerned. He didn't care how innocent the guy tried to appear, he was going to get the evidence and blow the whole thing out into the open. He would get to the bottom of the whole mystery if it took a month.

At last Del spoke up. "Know something, Phil?" he exclaimed, as though he had just realized what he was about to say. "As far as I can remember the location of that old house, the guy who made these tracks is headed right for it."

Phil reined up. "That's right. And we're getting pretty close to it. It's right over there on the rim of that gulch."

Doug rode up beside them. "You aren't figuring on going over to that old house, are you?" he asked uneasily.

"I've been thinking about it."

"You really mean that? You're going to barge up to it as though there's nobody around?"

"I just said I was thinking about going over there," Phil countered. "I didn't say anything about barging up to it as though there's nobody there." He paused. "That wouldn't be smart." He turned off the trail and headed in the direction of another part of the gulch.

"If we're thinking about doing the smart thing," Doug said, "we'd turn around and go back to the house, quick."

"Let's do the next smartest thing," Del put in.

Phil was only half listening. His gaze searched the

land ahead of them. "I think we'd better ride over to those trees and hide our horses so we can sneak up to the old house on foot."

Doug's eyes widened. "On foot?" he echoed. "Do you know what would happen to us if that guy, whoever he is, spies us around the house on foot? We'll be dead ducks for sure. Your dad won't even find enough of us left to write Danny and Kay and tell them what happened to us."

"That guy's not going to see us," Phil said confidently.

"I wish I could be as sure about that as you are," Doug said.

"Yeah," Del added, "wouldn't it be best for us to keep our horses so we can get away quick?"

"We'd never get close to that house on horseback," Phil reminded them. "We'd make as much noise as an army."

"Maybe so, but we could get away quick."

Nobody else said anything. They rode down the steep side of the gulch fifty yards or so to a place where the shrubs were the thickest.

Phil stopped and dismounted. "Come on, guys," he whispered. "We've got to hurry."

DeeDee gasped. "You aren't going to leave us here, are you?" she demanded.

"I thought maybe you'd rather stay here with the horses," Phil told her.

She shook her head vigorously. "You're not going

off and leave us here alone, that's all there is to it. Wherever you're planning on going, we're going along."

Del answered, "You can go along with us to the house if you want to." He grinned briefly. "Of course, if we should get caught–"

DeeDee and Marie looked at each other, hesitating.

"Well," Del continued, "make up your mind. What's it going to be?"

"Wh-wh-what do you want to do, Marie?" DeeDee asked.

"I don't know. What do you want to do?"

At that moment Phil spoke up. "I think the two of you had better stay here with the horses. We won't be gone more than a few minutes."

His sister's gaze sought his. "Are you sure?"

"All we're going to do is sneak over there as quietly as we can, take a look to see if the mysterious rider is staying there and then come back," Phil told her. "We probably won't be gone more than ten or fifteen minutes."

The girls reluctantly agreed to stay with the horses.

"But don't be long," DeeDee pleaded. "We'll wait for you here."

The boys tied their horses securely and disappeared in the direction of the old house. For the space of several minutes all was silent. Marie cleared her throat and turned slowly, peering into the brush, sure that someone was spying on them.

"I don't know about you," she said uneasily,

"but, DeeDee, I feel sort of creepy – like someone is watching us."

DeeDee didn't feel any calmer and more certain than her younger cousin, but she couldn't let Marie know that. She had to act as though she felt as safe as she did at the ranch house.

"There isn't any reason to be so upset," she said. "There's no one here except you and me."

"I suppose you're right." Marie spoke with some reluctance. "But I feel uneasy just the same. I'll be glad when the boys get back and we can get out of here."

DeeDee heard something in the mesquite to their right and jerked upright, smiling as she saw a long-legged jack rabbit go bounding out.

"If there was anybody around here, the boys wouldn't be of any help to us anyway," she went on. "They'd run faster than we would."

Marie glanced at her watch. "Just the same, I'd feel a whole lot better if they were back here and we were on our horses and started home." The words choked in her throat.

DeeDee stared at her, a spasm of fear seizing her. "Wh-wh-what–"

Marie's hand shook violently as she pointed. "Look over there!"

At that instant a slender, gray-haired man, his lean face bristling with whiskers, stepped out of the brush. He was older than Marie's dad, and he limped slightly.

"Howdy," he said. A brief smile lit up his wrinkled face.

The girls caught their breath and took half a step backward as though undecided whether to stand their ground or break and run.

"Don't you lay a hand on us!" DeeDee cried. In spite of the fierce hammering of her heart her voice was firm and clear. "I'm warning you! If you do, you'll have to answer to Uncle Clarence and he's a lot bigger'n you are."

A faint smile lifted one corner of the man's mouth. "Now, you can just simmer down, gal. I ain't fixin' to hurt you. I just got sort of lonesome and thought I'd come over and visit you for a spell."

The girls eyed him warily, but he made no move to come closer.

"Are–are you living in that old house?" Marie asked, still uneasy.

The man grinned. In spite of their fear the girls found themselves reassured by his smile.

"I reckon you might say that I'm camping there temporarily. Why?"

Neither DeeDee nor Marie answered him.

It was almost a minute before he spoke again. "How long have your friends been gone?"

DeeDee glanced helplessly at Marie and then back at the stranger. She didn't want to tell on Phil and her brothers, but she didn't want to lie to him either.

"F-f-friends? What friends?"

He laughed shortly. "Now don't tell me the two of you rode five horses over here," he said. When he continued, his voice lowered, and the girls squirmed uneasily. "What're they doing? Are they over there spying on my house?" He cackled again, as though it was one of the funniest jokes he had ever heard.

"Maybe I'd better get back over there so's they've got somebody to spy on. Must be mighty disgusting trying to spy on a fella when he ain't home."

DeeDee's temper flared. "You won't think it's so funny when the sheriff comes out and arrests you for killing that sheep."

The old man's eyes narrowed, glinting like cold steel in the morning sun. "What're you talking about, gal? I never killed no sheep in my life." His voice grated. "I may have felt like it a couple of times, but I never done it."

By this time DeeDee had grown braver. "Then who are you and what are you doing out here anyway?"

He answered in a slow drawl. "My name's Darrel Barrows, but my friends all call me Lefty."

He was still talking when the boys returned. They stopped, staring.

"Who's he?" Phil cried.

Lefty Barrows laughed. "Guess I should've waited to introduce myself. I could've saved some breath." He repeated his name and nickname and paused significantly. "Now who're you?"

Phil introduced himself, his sister, and the triplets.

Lefty pumped their hands vigorously, a grin splitting his face. "I'm right proud to know you." He paused. "I reckon seeing that old, abandoned house when I first rode in here was my lucky day. Yes, sirree, it sure was my lucky day."

"Maybe," Phil replied, speaking before he thought, "and maybe not."

Lefty Barrows' smile faded. "Now, what do you mean by that?"

Phil straightened, squaring his shoulders. It wouldn't do to let this stranger know everything.

"When I tell my dad about you camping out in that old house, he might not be so happy about it. He just might be so unhappy he'll drive you off."

The old cowhand squinted at him. "I don't run easy."

Marie spoke up quickly. "Dad might not say anything, Phil," she put in, "if we tell him how nice Lefty is. He might not care at all if he stays in the old house."

Barrows' eyes danced. "That's right. Your pa just might not get as worked up as you might think he's goin' to." He took half a step closer to Phil and spoke quietly. "Of course, we really don't have to tell him about me bein' out here, now do we? We don't have to let him know everything that's goin' on."

At first Phil didn't understand what he meant.

"Like your sister said," Lefty continued, "I ain't hurtin' nothin' out in the old house. There's no need of botherin' your dad about a thing like this. He's got too much on his mind to fool with it. Couldn't we just keep it a little secret?"

Phil frowned. "I can't do that," he said. "I don't keep anything from my parents, especially anything that has to do with the Circle R."

"Oh, come now. I know you don't always tell your dad everything that goes on. And you don't tell him the truth all the time neither."

The boy's eyes did not waver. "I used to lie to him," he said, "but not anymore."

Before the older man could ask about the reason for the change, Phil continued. "I'm a Christian now, and–" Moisture stood out on his forehead, and he fumbled uncertainly with the words. It wasn't easy to talk with someone about the reason he didn't lie anymore. "And the Bible says we shouldn't tell things that aren't true. So I've got to tell Dad that you're out here, whether I want to or not."

Disbelief crept into Lefty's faded eyes. "Well, I swan! That's the first time in all my born days that I ever heard a boy give a reason like that for not lyin'. I'm going to tell you somethin', young feller. Don't you ever let nobody talk you into tellin' somethin' that ain't true. I don't care if it's me or somebody else. It ain't right and you shouldn't ought to do it."

Marie broke in. "Let's go back to the ranch, Phil. We've been gone a long time."

"Do you have to leave so soon?" Disappointment

edged the old man's voice. "Seems as though you just got here."

"But we didn't bring any sandwiches or anything to eat," she continued, "and I'm getting hungry."

"We can take care of that pronto. Come with me and I'll fix you some sandwiches."

The kids hung back uncertainly.

"Come on. I'm a better cook than I look to be. Come on back to the house with me and I'll fix you up a regular old cowboy's meal like we used to fix when I was ridin' trail years ago. It'll stick to your ribs somethin' wonderful."

They went back to the old house with him. He built a little fire a dozen steps or so from the kitchen door and set to work. It was some time before he looked up at his young guests.

"Now, if you can wait until this fire gets to goin' a little better, I'll show you some eatin' that'll make your mouth water."

Lefty continued to talk as he worked. He told them what Texas was like when he was a boy, the sort of trouble they had herding cattle in the middle of the winter when the wind whistled in from the North, and what it was like at roundup time when they did the branding. The kids listened eagerly.

Lefty finished frying the bacon and eggs and opened a can of beans. He apologized for the can but said he had to get cans because it was easier.

"Only it don't taste like reg'lar wood-cooked beans.

No, sirree. They don't taste like wood- cooked beans at all. Guess that's one of the things I miss the most, the taste of the wood smoke in the beans."

The boys had not realized how hungry they were until they smelled the bacon sizzling in the frying pan. They and their sisters ate as though they hadn't eaten anything for a week.

"You were sure right about one thing." Doug smacked his lips. "That's the best bacon I ever ate."

"That's what I told you, ain't it? Nobody cooks bacon like Lefty Barrows. And that's a plumb, unadulterated fact."

Finally the time came for the kids to go. Only when they were in the saddle again did Lefty say anything to them about telling Clarence about him.

"You ain't changed your mind about squealin' on me to your pa, have you?"

Phil shook his head. "I'm sorry, but I've got to tell him."

"That's okay." There was resignation in his voice. "I just thought I'd check to find out for sure."

He still did not release his hold on the horse's reins. "There is one thing you could do for me, if you had a mind to," he continued.

"What's that?"

"When you tell your pa about me, you could put in a good word for me. You could tell him I ain't really hurtin' his old house none, and I'll clean it up good before I leave. You can do that, can't you?"

Phil nodded vigorously. "We sure can. And we will, believe me."

They rode a quarter of a mile or so away from the old house before anyone spoke. Finally Del turned to his cousin. "What do you think of Lefty Barrows, Phil?"

Before his cousin could answer, DeeDee spoke up. "I don't know about the rest of you, but I sort of liked him."

Phil thought a while before he spoke. "He seemed to be all right, but there's something sort of strange about him."

The others turned about to face him.

"What do you mean?" Doug asked. "What are you talking about?"

"I don't know for sure. There's just something about him that bothers me, and I don't know what it is."

CHAPTER 5

TURNABOUT

The boys and their sisters rode back toward the ranch buildings in silence. Doug glanced thoughtfully at Phil. He was usually quick to accept strangers, regardless of who they were or where they came from. Why would he feel so strange about the old cowboy? Lefty Barrows seemed like a real nice fellow. He didn't swear the way so many of the cowboys did, and he had been especially kind to the girls. Actually, he acted more like somebody's grandfather than a cowboy they had to be suspicious of.

At last Doug turned to Phil. "You must have some reason for being so suspicious of Lefty."

"It might not sound like much of a reason," Phil said in guarded tones, although they were far from the old house at the moment. "But it's sure got me wondering. When we were out back of the house, I took a look at his saddle."

"What about it?" Del broke in.

"You couldn't buy a saddle like that for five thousand dollars. And those boots of his must be worth at least five hundred dollars, maybe more."

The other boys whistled in amazement. "That is something," Doug observed.

But DeeDee and Marie were unimpressed by Phil's reasoning. They both came to the old ranch hand's defense.

"That isn't any reason to think he's not nice," Marie said.

"She's right," DeeDee added. "Lefty might have won his saddle in a rodeo. Or maybe he used to have lots of money but had so much bad luck he doesn't have it anymore. Having an expensive saddle and boots isn't against the law."

"No," Phil said, "it isn't against the law to have an expensive saddle and pair of boots, but if he's got enough money to buy stuff like that, why is he camping out in an abandoned house all by himself?"

Del turned the matter over in his mind. "There are some other things that don't add up either," he said.

Doug glanced his way. "Like what?"

"First of all, he claimed he didn't steal that sheep or kill it, and I believe him."

Phil nodded. "He doesn't look to me as though he'd steal anything. I believe him."

"And another thing," Del called over his shoulder. "He talked as though he hadn't been in the old house more than a few days, yet Uncle Clarence's cowhand claimed he saw lights out in the house almost two weeks ago."

"I'd never thought of that," Phil answered. "Now, maybe I can get Dad out here to look around!"

* * *

Clarence went thoughtfully back to his account books. Every now and again he laid his pen aside and looked up. He found Carmen more perplexing – and more lovable – every day since she got religious, or whatever it was that had happened to her.

He thought she would jump at a chance to get the triplets back, regardless of the way it had to be done. A year before she wouldn't have given a second thought to the fact that she had told the Orlises they could have custody of the triplets. She would have reasoned it away by claiming she had been so upset emotionally by her sister's death that she hadn't been thinking properly. Ever since he had known her, she had been the type of person who got what she wanted one way or another. And she hadn't let a little thing like her word or a few lies or some sharp angling by a smart attorney stand in the way.

This was something new. He tugged at the lobe of an ear. Maybe there was something to this religious bit after all. At least it seemed to have made some changes in Carmen's life, changes he hadn't thought would ever be made.

When the internet preacher came on later in the day, he stopped what he was doing and listened. He didn't go in the other room where Carmen was listening. That would let her know what he was doing and might give her the wrong idea. She might embarrass him with questions.

He remembered Rosalita and Jerry had talked about "salvation" the same way this preacher did when they came to visit. Thinking back, it seemed that was about the only thing they ever talked about. But he hadn't let it bother him. He had been able to explain the Bible away or simply ignore it.

But for some reason it was different now. As the speaker brought his message, the words went to the depths of his heart. *He* was the one the speaker was talking to. *He* was the sinner. Not some drunken saddle bum; not an alcoholic; not a wife-beater or a cattle thief; not somebody else whom respectable people looked down on, but *he*, Clarence Roper – rancher and father. A man who was looked up to in that part of Texas; the proud, arrogant Clarence Roper, who prided himself on being different from other men. He was the one who was going to an eternity without God unless he committed his life to the Lord Jesus Christ.

For the first time in his life Clarence realized that he wasn't different at all. He was made of the same weak, miserable piece of clay as other men. And he was going to hell if he didn't confess his sin and make his decision for Christ. The realization was staggering.

As soon as the speaker finished, Clarence got noisily to his feet. Carmen heard him and came to the door, disturbed by the pallor in his cheeks and the taut lines about his mouth.

"Where are you going, Clarence?" she asked curiously.

The old belligerence flashed. "Out!" he retorted, staring at her. Then, turning on his heel, he strode from the house.

As soon as Clarence was outside, he was sorry for the way he had talked to Carmen. He hadn't wanted to be rude. He just had to be alone. He had to get out where he could think things through. He didn't feel as though he could talk to anybody right then.

As he always did when he was disturbed about something, he went out to the barn, saddled Gentleman Joe, and rode out across the prairie in the opposite direction from that taken by the kids.

* * *

The triplets and Phil and Marie pushed their horses as much as they dared the rest of the way back to the ranch house. Sweat lathered their mounts' withers, and the horses were breathing heavily as they reached the barn.

Del turned to his cousin. "Hey, Phil, do you think your dad'll want to go out there tonight to see about Lefty Barrows?"

Phil dismounted. "I don't think he will unless he drives in the pickup. He won't want to go by horseback, as late as it is."

Clarence had come back from his ride and was unsaddling his horse when the kids entered the barn.

"Dad!" Phil cried, excitement lacing his voice.

"What's the trouble?" Clarence stopped what he was doing and whirled quickly.

"Dad, you've got to believe us this time. We've found the man who's living in the old house."

"Oh." The rancher turned slightly, keeping his eyes averted so the kids couldn't see the anguish that still smoldered there. Phil had said something about a man and the old house, but Clarence didn't actually understand what he was talking about. And, strangely, he didn't particularly care. There were far more important things troubling him at the moment.

His son read his disinterest and his excitement died. "Didn't you hear me, Dad? I said we found the guy who's been living in the old house along the gulch."

"That's good." His father spoke without enthusiasm.

"But you act as though you don't even care," Phil protested.

"Oh, sure I do." Clarence hunkered down just inside the barn. "But I don't have the slightest clue as to what you're talking about. Now suppose you start at the beginning and tell me exactly what happened."

Clarence forced himself to listen while Phil told how they had followed the tracks and found Lefty Barrows.

DeeDee broke in. "Actually, we didn't find Lefty. He found us."

Clarence did not reply.

"He didn't want us to tell you that he's out there, but I told him that I wouldn't keep anything from you," Phil went on.

His dad looked up. "Why did you tell him that?" he asked curiously.

"Because I–I'm a Christian and a Christian isn't supposed to lie or deceive."

Even that simple statement twisted like a flaming sword in Clarence's heart. First that day Carmen had shown him the changes that had come into her life, demonstrating them in a way he had not believed possible for her. Now Phil was doing the same thing. And neither knew about the other. This religion of theirs did make them odd, and he was sure he didn't like what had happened to them in many ways. But he had to admit that their religion had changed them. They were different than they had been before. Slowly he got to his feet.

"We'll have to go out and see about it tomorrow," he said.

The kids eyed him, disappointment chilling

them. This had not been the sort of reaction they had expected. They thought his temper would flare and that he would begin making plans to go storming out to question the intruder. They had even thought he would want to go out that very night to talk with Lefty.

Phil spoke again, his tone revealing his own disappointment. "Aren't you going to do something about it, Dad?"

"Of course," Clarence told him. "I said that I wanted to go out and talk to him, but I don't see any point in going tonight. There'll be time enough to make the trip in the morning."

"Dad," Marie said, breaking in, "when you go, can we go along?"

He eyed her quizzically. "I don't know about that. Your mother might have something else planned for you in the morning."

"Oh, we'll get up and take care of it before you go," she told him.

Clarence did not answer one way or the other.

He went into the house with them and sat at the table during dinner, but he ate only a few bites. That was unusual for him, especially when Carmen had fixed a thick beef roast with potatoes and gravy. Next to steak, that was his favorite meal, and, when Carmen served it, he was usually lavish with his praise. This time he said nothing.

Carmen noticed that he wasn't eating normally. "Don't you feel well?"

"Sure, I feel all right," he replied evasively. "I'm just not very hungry tonight."

After a few minutes he asked to be excused and pushed back from the table.

"You have to go somewhere, Clarence?" Concern flecked his wife's dark eyes.

He shook his head. "No farther than the den."

In the living room he stopped at the magazine rack and began to rummage through it. He had seen a book written by that preacher around the house someplace. Every once in a while, when he came in, Carmen was reading it.

He could get it easily enough by asking her where it was, but he could never do that. He didn't want to let her know that he was even aware she had it. It would only give her the wrong impression. After all, he wasn't getting serious about this religion of hers. He was just curious about it and wanted to find out if it explained why Carmen and Phil were so different now that they were Christians.

At last he located the book and took it to the den, closing the door securely. He sat down at his desk and began to read. The book wasn't what he thought it would be at all. It didn't have a stack of dos and don'ts the way he thought it would. And it didn't say he had to go to one particular church. Instead, it presented the claims Christ had on his life.

He read the book with great care. He had never before considered the things that were presented there. It both fascinated and repelled him. It would be wonderful to believe that way, to have a faith that was strong and all-sufficient to meet any emergency. Yet, it required much – too much, to his way of thinking.

Still, he was interested enough to get Carmen's Bible and begin to read it. She had underlined a good many places. He read some of those verses, but they cut even deeper than the book by the preacher.

Almost an hour later Carmen came timidly into the den and found him sitting motionless at his desk, staring blankly at the wall.

"You've been in here so long I've been worried, Clarence," she said. "I–" Carmen stopped suddenly as she saw the Bible open on the desk before him. "Excuse me. I'll–"

"No, wait!" His voice was harsh. "I want to talk to you."

She came back into the den and sat down near the desk, eyeing him carefully, but not daring to speak.

"Don't get any ideas, Carmen," he blurted, his irritation showing through. "I got to wondering about some things about this religion of yours, but I ain't getting any ideas about doing what you did. So you can forget it."

She nodded.

When he saw that she was not going to pressure him he continued.

"How does believing in Jesus save a person?" he wanted to know.

She thought for a moment, a prayer for wisdom in her heart.

"I don't really know how believing in Jesus can save anyone," she said. "I've never had it explained to me. But I know it does because I've experienced it in my own life."

She went on to explain the way of salvation in detail as best she knew how, quoting some of the Bible verses she had learned which emphasized her points. When she finished, Clarence leaned back in his chair, his gaze piercing.

"I'm not figuring on trying it," he protested. "I could never live up to any religion the way you and Phil do." There was a strange, wistful tone in his voice. "There wouldn't be any use in my trying."

Carmen was understanding. "I know how you feel," she said, "but you remember the bad temper I used to have, don't you?"

He smiled. "How could I forget it?" The whole county used to shake when you got mad."

"Did you ever think I could learn to control it?" she went on.

"Nope." The last trace of sarcasm faded from his voice. "That's one of the things that's made me see you've got something I don't have."

Carmen continued quietly. "Let me tell you about it, Clarence. If I had to depend on Carmen Roper,

I'd still be getting mad over every little thing that happens. But God knows how weak we are. So He helps us to live the way we should. We can't do it in our own strength."

This, too, was something that was new to Clarence. He had to think about it, to consider it from every angle.

If he followed Phil and Carmen, his rancher friends would howl with derision. Everywhere he went they would be laughing at him and his new stand. But that didn't matter to him right then. The only thing that really concerned him at the moment was the sudden realization that he was lost and headed for a Christless eternity, that he was missing out on the real joy and purpose of life.

He leaned forward earnestly. "Carmen, do you think God would save a guy like me?"

She nodded wordlessly, tears flooding her eyes and tracing down her olive cheeks. "I know He can, Clarence," she finally managed to say. "He saved me."

Together they knelt on the lush carpet. Under her guidance he murmured a disjointed, stumbling prayer, asking God's forgiveness.

For a time Carmen was stunned by what had happened. It didn't seem real, somehow, but was more like a dream, a strange and wonderful fantasy that could not possibly be true. Yet it was. Clarence was on his knees beside her. She could hear his labored breathing and feel the strength of his arm as it touched hers.

As the full reality of the event came upon her, she started to cry and could not stop. She had thought she had been so happy the day she committed her life to Christ that she could never equal that moment. But, if possible, this was greater. Clarence was a Christian! He had accepted the Lord Jesus Christ as his personal Savior. They would now have a truly Christian home.

Neither Carmen nor Clarence slept that night. They were awake talking until dawn began to light the prairie. Then they slipped out of bed, dressed, and read the Bible and prayed together.

When they had finished, Clarence closed the Bible thoughtfully and returned it to his desk. "You're sure going to have to help me to live the way I should, Carmen," he said. "I can't do it alone."

Her face glowed. "We'll help each other," she told him. "And God will help both of us."

Carmen hoped he would tell the kids at the breakfast table that morning, but he said nothing about what had happened to him. Neither did Carmen, feeling the news should come from him.

As soon as they sat down to eat, Phil turned to his father. "Are you all set to go out to the old house this morning, Dad?"

"You're not going to let me rest until you drag

me out there, are you?" But a smile played over Clarence's face.

"We want you to meet this Lefty Barrows," Phil said. "He's really a nice guy."

Marie reached over impulsively and laid a hand on her father's arm. "You aren't going to kick him out, are you, Dad?"

"Don't you think I should?"

"No," she retorted. "He's nice."

"But you know how I feel about having squatters on my land," he persisted. Marie missed the twinkle in his blue eyes.

"He's not hurting anything by living out there, Dad," she said. "He's got the house all cleaned up, and he's nailed some boards over the broken windows."

"Well, we'll see."

Clarence had intended to go out to the old house with them, but just as they were saddling their horses to leave, a cattle buyer came unexpectedly, and Clarence felt that he had to stay there.

"Why don't you boys ride out and tell this friend of yours to come in and talk to me," he suggested. "If he looks all right to me, we'll see if we can work out something so he can stay out there for a while."

Marie spoke quickly. "It's all right if DeeDee and I go along with Phil and Doug and Del, isn't it?"

"I guess you can ride along if you want to."

The boys frowned, and DeeDee and Marie smirked

triumphantly. This was one time the boys weren't going to be able to run off from them.

They finished saddling up and together they rode across the hills. Phil had noticed the change that had come over his dad.

"Did you think Dad acted funny?" he wanted to know.

"I don't know," Del replied. "What do you mean?"

"I don't know either, but he didn't act like himself at all."

Marie nodded her agreement. "I noticed he acted different about Lefty than I thought he would," she said. "I don't believe he's going to make him leave."

"It was more than that," Phil continued. "I don't know what it is, but he sure doesn't act the way he did before."

"Maybe he doesn't feel good," Doug suggested.

Phil didn't think it was that, but he didn't press the subject further. For the next few minutes, he was wrapped in thought.

It didn't seem to take nearly as long for them to ride back to the deserted house the second time. When they got there, Lefty was out in back. He waved to them as soon as they were in sight.

"Hi, Lefty," Doug sang out in his haste to beat the others with the information. "We've got some news for you."

The old cowhand acted as though he hadn't even

heard them. "You didn't happen to see an empty corn sack as you came this way?"

They shook their heads.

"No, why?" Phil asked.

"I don't mean to be accusin' you or anything like that, but the sack of corn I brought along to feed my horse is gone! And I haven't fed half of it to him!"

"Gone?" Phil echoed, surprise widening his eyes. "It couldn't be!"

"You just come here an' look around for yourself, young feller. You won't see hide nor hair of any sack of corn. It's been stole! And not by no varmints either. Leastwise it wasn't the four-legged kind."

"But there isn't anybody around here who would steal your corn. The closest people live at the ranch and nobody from there took it. I can tell you that."

Lefty pushed his hat back on his head and scratched his ear. "That's what I figgered," he said. "There just ain't nobody around here to steal that corn, so it couldn't have been taken by anyone. But you can look for yourself! It's been stole, all right! Anybody can see that it had to be!"

CHAPTER 6

BLUE WRECK

After Clarence finished his business with the cattle buyer and they had a cup of coffee, he saddled his horse and rode out to the old, abandoned house to meet Lefty. He had told the kids to have the old man come in to the ranch house with them, but he got uneasy and went out there himself.

Phil, Marie, and the Davis triplets were out back talking with Lefty when Clarence rode up and dismounted.

"You must be Lefty, the man the kids have been telling me so much about," he said, striding forward and thrusting out his hand.

"Right you are," Lefty exclaimed, cocking his head to one side and squinting at Clarence. "Lefty Barrow's my name."

Clarence acknowledged the introduction, and introduced himself.

"How about comin' in an' settin' for a spell?" Lefty asked. "I could flip up a cup of coffee in a hurry."

"I'd like to," Clarence told him, "but I don't have time. I'm running behind this morning."

Lefty was surveying Clarence critically, trying to measure the rancher's attitude toward him.

"Suit yourself, but I make a tolerable good pot of coffee."

"I'll have to take a rain check on that. I just came out here this morning because the kids wanted me to see you."

The old man nodded. "That figgers." He drew himself up to his full height and stared into Clarence's eyes. "Now that you've seen me, what're you fixin' to do? Run me off your land?"

Clarence straightened thoughtfully. "I don't know for sure," he said. "To tell you the truth, I don't know whether that would solve anything or not."

"Well," Lefty said, squinting, "it would get me out of your old house, if that's botherin' you."

There was a brief silence. "You aren't hurtin' anything, are you?"

A strange gleam flickered in the old cowboy's eyes. "I don't reckon I am. Leastwise, I sure don't figger on hurtin' anything."

"Well, then, I don't see why there'd be any point in runnin' you off."

Lefty gasped. "You–you mean you ain't goin' to make me leave?" he asked.

Clarence grinned. "I don't see any good reason for asking you to go."

The grizzled old cowhand shook his head. "Y'know, I just about rolled up my sleepin' bag and skedaddled. You sure ain't what I figgered I'd be runnin' into when that kid of yours said he was goin' to tell you that I was out here."

Clarence's gaze met his. "I'll tell you something, Lefty," he said. "If I'd come out here yesterday, you'd have gotten the boot, but good!"

The old man's face twisted. "And just exactly what changed things in such an all-fired hurry?"

The rancher's face softened, and for a fleeting instant, it appeared that he was about to continue. Then he changed his mind. "I'll tell you all about it sometime."

They talked for several minutes before the rancher glanced at his watch and announced that he had to leave.

"I'd like to sit and jaw with you for a spell," Lefty said. "Stop by again when you've got the time."

"I'll do that."

Lefty followed him back to his horse. "And if you see any strangers around here," the old man went on, "I'd be obliged if you'd let me know about it. There's someone 'round here got sticky fingers. He stole my corn."

Clarence started back to the ranch with the kids but changed his mind when they were half a mile or so from the abandoned house. He reined up and told Phil that he wouldn't be going any further with them. He was going to ride over to the Lazy S to talk with Glen Porter about something.

"I've got to tell him about what happened to me last night."

His son's eyes widened curiously.

"What do you mean, Dad?"

"I'll tell you all about it sometime." He lifted the reins, and his horse, sensing that he was about to be off, began to fiddle-foot expectantly. "Glen's the toughest guy around here," he muttered. "I figure he's the best place to start."

With that he clucked to his wiry cow pony, and the horse burst into a gallop.

The kids remained motionless on their saddle horses for a minute or two, watching him as he rode away.

"What do you suppose he was talking about?"

Doug and Phil both shook their heads. "I sure couldn't get it," Doug observed. "First he told Lefty that if he had come out to the old house yesterday he'd have run him off, but today he didn't even seem mad at the old guy. And now he says he's got something to talk to Glen Porter about, and he's the toughest guy around here, so that's the best place to start. It doesn't make sense to me."

Suddenly lights gleamed in DeeDee's eyes. "You know what I think? I think he's become a Christian!"

Phil drew his breath sharply.

"Do you suppose he has?" he asked. It was as though he couldn't quite believe that such a miracle could happen, that his dad would turn his life over to the Lord Jesus Christ.

Marie said nothing. Her olive face was ashen and a strange, cold fire gleamed in her snapping black eyes. If that was true, she was the only one of the little group who wasn't a believer. But that was something that couldn't happen. Her dad would never desert her that way! He would never make a decision for Christ after he had talked so terribly about those who had already become Christians. No, there had to be some other explanation.

They were still discussing the possibility as they began to ride toward the ranch house once more. After a time, Del noticed that they were going a slightly different direction, but he didn't say anything about it for a while. Actually, he had assumed that Phil had decided on going home another way.

Phil's eyes were focusing on the hills around them, but he wasn't really seeing them. He was thinking about his dad. He had heard him rail against God in a way he had never heard anyone else do. He had seen his lips tighten and his anger flame until he seemed to lose control of himself. How could a man like that give his heart to Christ?

The fact that Phil and his companions were off

the trail didn't register until they reached a narrow mesquite-clogged gulch that was unfamiliar.

He reined up suddenly. "Wait a minute!"

Doug and Del both came up beside him. "Where are we?" Doug asked.

A sheepish grin lifted the corners of Phil's mouth. "If I told you," he said, "you'd think I'd gone out of my mind."

Marie frowned. "Phil!" she exclaimed irritably. "Do you know where we are?"

"We're not where we're supposed to be, by a long shot. I can tell you that much."

DeeDee turned to him. "I thought you were one of those guys who never got lost or off the trail. I thought you told me you were a natural-born tracker."

Her cousin laughed. "The trouble is, we're not tracking now," he said. "And what I meant is that I almost never get off the trail."

Del glanced up at the sun that was scribing a blistering arc across the pale sky. "We'd better hurry," he said, "or your dad's going to finish his errand and beat us back to the ranch. He'll be wondering what happened to us."

"He'll have a good idea," Marie retorted. "He knows what a 'good' tracker Phil is."

"Well, come on," her brother said. "We've got a lot of riding to do."

Still Marie did not move. "We can't cross the

gulch through that stickery mesquite. We'll ruin our clothes and get all scratched up besides."

Doug turned in his saddle and shaded his eyes with his hand. "What're you figuring on, Phil?" he asked. "Are we going to have to ride all the way back where we came from?"

"Nope." The boy's irritation had begun to show through. "We're only about half a mile from the highway. We'll ride over to it, cross the gulch on the highway bridge, and come back on the other side. That'll beat going all the way back."

They were within sight of the highway when Phil saw an old car pushed into the mesquite on the opposite side of the gulch. He reined to a halt.

"Look at that, would you?" he exclaimed. "I don't think I've ever noticed that over there."

"That's a funny place to park," DeeDee said.

"It looks to me as though it quit running and someone pushed it over there to hide it," Del observed.

They crossed the bridge and galloped along the opposite side of the gulch until they reached the car. Whoever had gotten it off the road had taken some pains to hide it. It was pushed back in the mesquite until it was not visible from the highway. Only by going along the gulch could it be seen.

"It sure is an old wreck," Doug said, dismounting and going over to the vehicle.

It was an old sedan that had once been blue but was now almost completely devoid of paint. Fenders, bumpers, and doors showed the ravages of repeated accidents. One rear tire was blown out and the other was flat. There was a thin trail of oil from the highway to the place where the car stood.

"I don't think anybody's going to drive this for a while." Del said.

His brother moved to the other side, noting the wrinkled fenders and other obvious signs of abuse.

"If you ask me," he put in, "nobody's going to drive this old wreck again, ever. I think it's about had it."

Phil continued to move around the old car, examining it carefully. There weren't any license plates on it, and from the rusted bolts that were still in place, it was apparent there hadn't been any plates on it for a number of years. Yet the tracks indicated that it had been driven or pushed off the road recently.

"This is a mystery," Phil said thoughtfully.

Del laughed. "If a car ran on corn," he said, "we'd know where Lefty's sack of corn went."

DeeDee went back to her horse and remounted. "I don't think there's anything so mysterious about it," she said. "Somebody was driving this old wreck down the highway when it quit running. So they got disgusted and pushed it over here. That's about all there is to it."

Doug was not entirely satisfied, and neither was Phil.

"Maybe," her cousin said uneasily. "And maybe not."

DeeDee was disgusted with them. They would stand and look at that old car all day when anyone could see what happened without getting all worked up about it. If it was anything but a car, they wouldn't be half so interested in it. Next thing, they would be wanting to get it back to the ranch so they could see if they could make it run.

"Well," she said, "we'd just as well get on our way. We aren't going to accomplish anything by standing out here looking at that old pile of junk."

Phil grinned up at her. "And besides," he finished for her, "you'd like to get back to the ranch, wouldn't you?"

"How did you guess it?"

"Listen, I've got a sister. I know how her mind works. I know exactly how it works."

They were getting on their horses when Marie saw a sudden movement in the mesquite just over the lip of the gulch. Her eyes bugged and her lower jaw sagged slightly.

"Marie!" DeeDee cried. "What is it?"

For answer Marie pointed a trembling finger. Her mouth worked, but no words came out.

DeeDee stared in the direction Marie was pointing, but all she could see was the gray, gnarled fingers of mesquite and the saber-sharp blades of Spanish sword.

"I don't see anything," she blurted.

By this time the frightened girl had found her voice. "S-s-somebody is watching us!" she cried. "Right over there!"

CHAPTER 7

MACK

Diminutive twelve-year-old Mack Flores had been at the bottom of the gulch gathering dry wood for his mother to use in baking tortillas when he heard the riders clattering across the highway bridge. At first he didn't pay much attention to them. There wasn't a great deal of traffic along the highway, but there was enough, so it wasn't startling to hear someone. But when they left the main road and came back along the other side of the gulch, he stopped what he was doing and listened intently.

Moisture beaded his dark forehead, and he wiped it away with a firm hand. He hoped Mama and the younger kids were out of sight as he had told them to be. It wouldn't do to let anyone see them.

He wasn't quite sure why he felt that way, and he hadn't been able to answer his young brother

Eduardo when he wanted to know why they had to hide all the time.

"We didn't have to hide when we were home," he had protested.

"But we're not home now." That wasn't any answer, but it was the best he could do.

Mama, who had been busy over the open fire frying tortillas, had looked up.

"Now, Eduardo," she said, her voice firm as she spoke in Spanish, "you know we all agreed that we would do what Mack says without asking any questions."

"But–"

"Mack is right," she repeated. "It is not good that anyone sees us."

Mack had drawn himself up to his full four feet ten inches. Tears smarted in his black eyes, but he tried to hold them back, to keep them from trickling down his cheeks. To hear Mama talk that way, saying that he was the man of the family now that Papa was dead, made him so proud he thought his heart would burst. But the fear came too, stealing in to grasp him with its icy fingers.

He was proud to be the man of the family and have his brothers and sisters, and even Mama, look to him when it came time to decide what they should do. But it was hard. He had never thought how hard it could be to be the papa and have to say what to do and what not to do. It would be so much easier to follow what somebody else said.

Mama and his brothers and sisters ate so many tortillas and tacos. And it took more cornmeal than he could get to keep them from being hungry all the time. Mama had said that most of the cheese was gone now. That meant no more enchiladas. And there was no more milk for the baby.

If they had just had some money, they could get anything they needed in this grand country of Texas. Or, if they could find Mama's cousin Hernandez, he would help them. In Mexico a man was trained to help the members of his family. It was the way of their people.

But Mack didn't know for sure where Hernandez lived, and Texas was so big. And the old car they drove up from Brownsville was so leaky in the motor and so weak in the tires that it would go no more. They had to stay there. Mama could not walk and carry the baby, and a couple of the little ones were too small to go more than a mile or so. He didn't have any choice but to remain where they were.

Mack Flores held his breath and listened. Whoever was up there had stopped beside the old car. The boy's pulse quickened. Maybe whoever it was would find out about Mama and the children and him.

Stealthily Mack picked his way through the tangled mass of mesquite, his bare feet ignoring the sharp stubble. As quietly as a cub jaguar, he made his way up the steep bank, careful to keep a clump of mesquite between him and whoever was up there poking around the car.

It was then that Marie had seen him and had cried out in fear. Mack had been as frightened as she. He flattened against the ground, the breath freezing in his lungs.

"Marie!" Phil cried, "can't you quit that stuff? You'll have us all thinking there's someone hiding behind every tree."

"But, Phil, I–"

"I know. I know. You saw somebody ten feet tall who's going to catch us and stomp us into the ground all the way up to our ears."

The scoffing American voice floated down to Mack. It was a voice he could understand somewhat from those glorious days when Papa had taken the family north to work in the beet fields. Mama hadn't learned any English then. She didn't listen to them when they talked it and didn't try to understand. When she wanted to know what had been said, she asked her husband or Mack to tell her. She said she was much too busy and, besides, it was too hard for her.

Mack was glad he and Papa had learned a little English. Now he could understand enough to know that the young Americano did not believe the one called Marie when she said she saw someone hiding in the brush. Mack breathed deeply. At least they hadn't gotten a good look at him. His secret was still safe.

"Come on!" Phil exclaimed again to his sister. "We've got a long ride ahead of us."

Still Marie was not satisfied. "But I–"

"Come on! We've got to get back to the ranch. We can't fool around here all day."

While Mack crouched in his hiding place the visitors remounted and went galloping off. Only when the sound of pounding hooves died away in the distance did he relax enough to get to his feet.

He made his way back to the bottom of the gulch and gathered an armload of dry wood. Carefully he approached the bridge. Nobody would have guessed that Mama and he had fixed a shelter for the family under the highway bridge. They had found a few old planks that had been discarded when the new bridge was built, enough to make a side and one end. The other end was filled with mesquite and mud. A tattered blanket served as a door.

Making the shelter had taken almost a week, even with the help of the younger children. But now it was done and was almost as tight as the shack they had been living in in Brownsville.

Mama knew how to build a fire so there was hardly any smoke. A person would have to be looking for smoke to see the tiny spiral from her tortilla fires. Mack felt confident that they would not be discovered. Yet the happenings of the last few minutes were unsettling.

He was still thinking about the matter when

Eduardo came rushing out to meet him. He was two years younger than Mack, a dark, bright-eyed boy with shaggy hair and an appealing smile.

"Did you see them, Mack?" he asked.

"*Sí*." He tried to act as Papa would have acted if one of the kids questioned him, calm and unafraid and wise about everything.

"I was scared, Mack. When they stopped at the old car, I was so scared I hardly breathed. You think maybe they will find us, Mack?"

The older boy shook his head gravely. "They've gone home to the ranch," he said, quoting Phil. "Wherever that is."

Mama was frying tortillas when he came up with the wood. She too wanted to know about the riders who stopped to examine the old car.

"You think they will cause trouble, Mack?" she asked, concern in her voice. "You think they will find us?"

He shook his head. "They won't find us. They didn't listen to the girl who tried to tell them that she saw me."

Mama seemed relieved but only for a moment. She turned the last tortilla and looked up at her oldest son uneasily.

"The corn is almost gone, Mack," she told him, fear creeping into her voice.

"Almost gone?" he exclaimed. A deadly chill took hold of him. "So soon?"

"*Sí*. I tried to make it last, but there are many mouths to feed."

Mack went over to the doorway of their improvised shelter and sat down. He had been fortunate to find the lamb and later the sack of corn. It had kept the younger children's stomachs full for a time. But the meat had long since been gone, and now there was very little corn.

That meant he had to do something. He was the one who had to bring home the corn for the tortillas and the meat or cheese and milk. There had to be milk for the baby.

Mack's mother had said nothing about the milk, but that was not because there was no need. It was just that there was no way for Mack to get any milk, as badly as the little one needed it. Instead, she had cooked some of the tortilla meal in water and fed it to the baby, hoping it would be enough to keep her little body healthy.

Mack leaned back against the mud wall. Maybe he could go to this ranch the riders had talked about and work to earn a little money or another sack of corn. Or they might have a scrawny lamb nobody wanted or a chicken.

But there was a problem in going to the ranch. They would be wanting the answers to all sorts of questions about where he came from and where his family was and how he came to be so far from town.

No, it wouldn't do for him to appear at the ranch. That could ruin everything.

Slowly the boy got to his feet. He would have to think of something else. It might be better to go back to that old building where he got the corn. There he would only have one man to watch out for. He ought to be able to sneak back to the barn and see if there was anything else around that could be used to feed the family.

It would be worth a try anyway. If he waited around until he was sure the old man had gone somewhere, he might even be able to get into the house. And if he could do that, he ought to find a lot of things to eat. Just thinking about it brought a wide smile to his face. Wouldn't Eduardo and his sisters and brothers open their eyes if he came back with meat and potatoes and corn? They would know, then, how well he could take care of them.

While he stood there deliberating what to do, one of his younger sisters came over to him, her eyes gazing somberly into his. She didn't speak. She didn't have to. He knew what she was thinking. It was the way she would have looked at Papa if he were there. Those sad eyes were whispering that she was hungry, that there were not enough tortillas to take away the hurt in her stomach. She wasn't complaining. She just looked up at him with trust and hope, knowing that he would do what he could.

* * *

It had been hard for Mama and Mack and his brothers and sisters since Papa died. He might have lived, the doctor said, if there had been a hospital in their little Mexican village. But there was none and so he continued to get worse until he died.

Mama had kept the family together and tried to see that they had food and clothing, but there was never enough to go around. The others in the village helped when they could, but they often went hungry too.

Then Mama had remembered Cousin Hernandez who lived far away in Texas. "We will go to see Hernandez," she announced. "He will help us."

It frightened Mack to think of going anywhere, but they had to do something. In their own little village, he would never be able to get enough together for the family to eat.

"*Sí,*" he said. "It is good. We will go to see Cousin Hernandez."

They got a few pesos together by selling some of their belongings and went north to Matamoros. They had thought they would get to cross the bridge as easily as they did when Papa was with them when they went north to work, but something was different this time. Mack tried to explain about the kids needing something to eat and about going to Cousin

Hernandez who would help them, but it didn't make any difference. They could not go to Texas.

One of the men they met in Matamoros explained it all to Mama. She didn't understand a great deal of what he said, only the part about Charro Days.

"We can cross the bridge then, Mack," she told him. "We have only to wait."

Fortunately, the time for Charro Days was almost upon them. They waited, scrounging food from first one family that was almost as destitute as they were and then from another. A little cornmeal here, some cheese from someone else. Another woman shared what little milk she had with Mama so she could feed the little one.

With the first crowd of visitors to Brownsville for Charro Days, they crossed the bridge into Brownsville. But still they were not where Cousin Hernandez lived.

"We will have to walk there."

Mama carried baby Carmelita, and the others walked beside her and Mack. They would have been in great trouble right from the first if some kind señor had not told them about the soldiers.

"You have to wait until they stop guarding the roads or bad things will happen to all of you, señora," he said. "It is better that you wait."

Then, because he felt sorry for her, he helped her get a job washing dishes in a little restaurant. Another Mexican family took them in. Mama used great care with her money, and when the time came that she no longer had a job, she bought an old car, had one of the boys show Mack how to drive it, and they set out to find Cousin Hernandez.

* * *

Mack kicked at a stone with his foot. They had been all right as long as the car went, but now it had quit. What should he do?

CHAPTER 8

THIEF!

Phil led his sister and their cousins along the arroyo away from the abandoned car at a brisk trot. Marie must have been wrong about seeing somebody hiding in a clump of mesquite near that old junk heap. Nobody would have been in that area yet, and if they had been, they wouldn't have been hiding. They'd have been glad enough somebody came along. Still, Marie's insistence bothered him.

When they stopped to rest their horses, Phil questioned his sister pointedly. Marie was vague, but he could not shake her. She was convinced she had seen someone.

"You probably saw something move in the mesquite and imagined that it was someone," he said.

She frowned and shook her head emphatically. "No, I didn't. It was someone moving in the brush. I know it."

Doug spoke up. "You know," he said, "Lefty Barrows enjoys a good joke as much as anybody. You don't suppose he saw where we were headed and sneaked over here to try and scare us, do you?"

Phil shook his head. "He couldn't possibly have gotten over here quick enough to hide in the gulch without our seeing him."

"I don't think it was Lefty either," Marie continued. "But I know it was somebody. If you had just taken the time to ride down there, you would have found his tracks and proved that I'm right."

"Maybe." Doubt still edged Phil's voice.

When they got back to the ranch house Clarence still was not there, but he rode in while they were unsaddling their horses. He still seemed to be preoccupied.

"Take care of my horse, Phil," he said, swinging to the ground and handing the reins to his son. "I've got to talk to your mother."

Clarence and Carmen were seated across from each other at the kitchen table when the kids entered the house. Phil was the first to burst through the door, with the others close behind.

"Hi, Mom!" he sang out. "What's for supper?" She did not answer him.

"Hey!" His smile fled as he looked from one to the other. "What's the matter? Did something happen?"

Carmen swallowed the lump in her throat and dabbed her eyes with a tissue.

"Dad has something to tell you," she said.

A strange, unnatural embarrassment took hold of Clarence. "Maybe you'd better tell 'em, Carmen," he said gruffly.

She shook her head.

He waited, but when he saw that she wasn't going to speak he cleared his throat and began.

"Well, like I told you, I went over to talk with Glen Porter."

Phil could stand the suspense no longer. "About what?" he demanded.

"I'm coming to that. I figured he was just about the toughest guy in this part of Texas and, if I could talk to him, I could talk to anybody."

He paused for a moment.

"So I went over and—and told him that I–I had accepted Christ as my Savior."

As he spoke Marie's dark eyes widened and the color drained from her cheeks. But the others were so excited and happy they didn't notice her reaction.

"I knew there was something different about you, Dad," Phil said, "when we rode out to the old house with you."

It was Clarence's turn to beam.

They sat in the kitchen for a long while talking about the Lord. Clarence told how the neighboring rancher had received him and how he acted when he told him of his decision to follow Christ.

"I thought he'd laugh at me, but he didn't. He

got real serious and asked me quite a few questions. When I left, he asked me to come back and talk to him again."

* * *

Carmen was happier than anyone could remember. There was a perpetual smile on her face and, as she worked, she hummed one of the songs she had heard on the preacher's program.

Instead of having their family devotions in one of the bedrooms so it would not be an offense to Clarence, they had them around the kitchen table. Clarence was responsible for that. That first night after he was saved, he had Doug get the Bible and read a passage from it. Then he stumbled haltingly through a prayer. When he finished, he turned apologetically to Carmen.

"I don't know much about this praying business, so I might not do it right. But the way I figure, if a man's a Christian, he ought to be able to lead his family in talking to God."

Carmen reached out impulsively and took his big hand in hers. "I don't think I've ever heard a more beautiful prayer in my life," she told him.

Clarence knew that she wasn't referring to the words of his prayer but to the fact that he had finally met God's conditions so he could pray.

* * *

The kids were so busy around the ranch the next few days they didn't even think about Lefty or the stranger Marie had thought she saw hiding near the old car.

Toward the end of the week Carmen decided it would be nice to invite Lefty to the ranch for Sunday dinner. She asked Clarence about it.

"It's all right with me," he said. "I enjoy talking with the old guy. But the kids would have to go out and invite him. I don't have the time to do it."

DeeDee spoke first. "We could go!" she exclaimed quickly.

Her uncle pursed his lips. "I suppose you could, at that."

"Hey!" Doug said. "What about us?"

His sister made a little face at him. "Marie and I don't have to have you along," she said. "We can ride out there ourselves. We know the way."

"If we don't go along, you'll get lost or get into trouble."

"I don't think we have to worry about anything like that, Doug," Clarence said. "Besides, I've got some things I want you guys to do today."

Doug groaned and the girls smirked.

As soon as the breakfast dishes were done, DeeDee and Marie packed a lunch and rode out to the old house. Once they were on the way, Marie wasn't too sure she wanted to go without one of the boys.

"I'd feel a lot better if they were with us," she said.

DeeDee snorted scornfully. "Oh, pooh! We don't have to have them along to take care of us."

"But what if–what if we come across that person who was hiding around that old car?"

"We don't have to worry about him. He's a long way from the old house, and he's not going to be going over where anybody is. He won't want to take a chance of being seen."

They rode on in silence. DeeDee wasn't actually as brave as she professed to be. When she got to thinking about the car and the man Marie might have seen there, she got weak in the knees. What if he had gone over to the house? What if Lefty had gone away somewhere and this other person was waiting for them when they got there? A shudder tingled up and down her spine.

But they couldn't go back, she told herself, not when the boys would laugh at them for it. No, they had to go on to see Lefty. DeeDee clucked impatiently to her horse and tried not to think about all the things that could happen to them.

When they rode up to the old house, Lefty was not in sight. Marie glanced about quickly, her uneasiness growing.

"Do you think he's here?" she asked.

DeeDee shook her head. "He's always come out to meet us as soon as we rode up the other times we've come here," she replied.

At that instant there was a tapping noise at the kitchen window.

"DeeDee!" Marie spoke in a hoarse whisper.

The girls stared at the familiar whiskered face in the window. Lefty was motioning to them.

"What does he want, DeeDee?" she asked.

"I think he wants us to ride around to the other door."

Lefty was waiting for them at the front door. He came out quickly, his faded blue eyes taking in the entire scene.

"Put your horses back in the mesquite out of sight," he said hoarsely, "and get in the house, quick."

"What for?" Marie demanded.

"I'll tell you later."

They did as they were directed. Once they stepped into the old house, he closed the door and hurried to the kitchen window where they had first seen him standing a moment or two before. Lefty stationed himself where he could get an unobstructed view of the barn.

DeeDee said curiously, "What's this all about?"

Lefty took a deep breath. "Do you girls remember that sack of corn somebody stole from me?"

The girls nodded.

"Well, yesterday I saw some tracks leadin' up to the house, like as though I might've scared some-body away."

DeeDee and Marie leaned forward intently. "Yes?"

"Well, I decided to bait me a trap," the old man went on. "This morning I made a big show of taking another sack of corn out to the barn. And two or three times I went out and got some. Now, I figure maybe that character what stole it is about to sneak back out there and get some more corn. And when he does, I'm going to catch me a thief!"

Lefty stopped talking suddenly. "Hey!" His voice lowered to a whisper. "What's going on out there, anyway?" Even as they watched, the barn door began to open stealthily. Someone who didn't belong there was in the barn!

For a brief, tension-packed instant the girls and Lefty stared out the window. They could not move. They could scarcely breathe. While they stared, a faded piece of blue denim appeared a foot or so above the doorsill.

DeeDee grasped Marie's arm. "Somebody's coming out!"

There was a short hesitation, and the piece of denim began to increase in size until it became the leg of a pair of blue jeans. The slight bulk in the doorway continued to increase in size until they could see a slender, dark-skinned young figure.

"A kid!" Lefty dashed for the door as fast as his arthritic legs could carry him. "Come on! We've got to get him before he gets away!"

Somehow the presence of the old ranch hand brought courage to the girls. They sped past Lefty in their mad dash for the barn. The boy who had come out of the dilapidated building seemed unable to move as DeeDee and Marie bore down upon him. He stood there, his gaze fixed on them as they dashed up.

It was only when Lefty neared that he tried to break and run. But he was too late. The old man dashed up to him as he turned to scamper away. His hand snaked out with surprising speed, and his fingers clamped on the boy's frail shoulder.

"Now, stand where you are and don't give me no trouble! You hear me?"

Fear widened Mack Flores's dark eyes. The strength seemed to seep from his body, leaving him limp and helpless.

"I–I don't do nothing'!" In his fright, his English was so broken they could scarcely understand him.

"Don't give me that guff!" Lefty roared. "You're the one who stole my sack of corn, and you'd have taken everything in the house that you could get your fingers on iffen I hadn't come back an' surprised you before you got away."

Mack stared numbly up into the whiskery old face. This was something he hadn't counted on. He had seen the old man around the buildings and he figured he might come back and catch him in the house, but he had thought he would be able to run fast enough to get away from him.

Mama and the little ones looked to him to get something for them to eat. Only that morning they had used the last of the corn to make tortillas and he hadn't been able to find another lamb or a cow that he could milk. They were depending on him to find food for their stomachs. He had to do something. And now he had ruined everything.

Mack tore his gaze away from Lefty's face and looked blankly at DeeDee and Marie. His temper blazed. Why should they have plenty to eat when his sisters and brothers went hungry?

Lefty's voice was harsh. "What did you do with my corn? Why did you steal from me?"

Mack did not answer him immediately. He didn't want to tell the old man something that wasn't true. Among his people gray hair and wrinkles were treated with respect. When an old man questioned, a boy answered. It was as simple as that.

He didn't want to speak a lie either. Mama and Papa had always told him to say straight out how things were, no matter what happened. And Mack had always followed their example in regard to telling the truth. But this was different. They didn't know about this man whose eyes seemed to pierce deep into Mack's heart, this old man with the fingers of steel that bit into his shoulder. He had not lied because he wanted to. He could not help it.

"I–I–no take nothing!"

Lefty drew back his other fist menacingly as though he was about to hit Mack and send him sprawling. The frightened boy cringed and tried to pull away.

"It ain't goin' to do you no good to lie," Lefty rasped, "and it ain't goin' to help to try to get away from me, young feller. So you'd just as well tell me the truth. How come you stole my corn?"

Mack cleared his throat. The words croaked out.

"I–I was just looking around," he said, his voice quavering. "I didn't figure on taking nothing. See!" He held out his hands so the old man could see that they were empty. "I never took nothing!"

Lefty snorted indignantly. "You mean you never got out of the barn with anything." Lefty was angry now because the boy would not admit what he had done. "You started out with another sack of my corn! That's what you were doin' in there! But when you saw that you were goin' to get caught you dropped it just inside the door!"

He pointed to the sack and the corn that was spilled on the ground.

"Now, s'pose you quit your lyin' an' tell me what this is all about before I lose my temper and give you a good whuppin'!"

Mack saw that he had been found out and that it would do no good to lie anymore. He nodded weakly, moistening his lips with the tip of his tongue.

"What you do to me?" he asked fearfully.

"That depends on what kind of a story you've got for me. Just what're you doin' with all this corn?"

CHAPTER 9

CAPTURE

Lefty still would not let Mack go. He ordered the Mexican boy inside the barn where he could watch him.

"Get in here and be quick about it!"

Fear flickered in the boy's eyes. "Why you want me in there?" he asked uneasily.

"So's I can keep an eye on you while I saddle my horse. That's why. I'm going to take you to the Circle R ranch house and let Clarence Roper decide what to do with you. That's what I'm going to do."

At the realization that he would have to face still another man, Mack's cheeks paled.

"Do you think he–he put me in jail?" His voice broke.

"That'll be up to Mr. Roper. I don't know what he'll do! But I can tell you this much, he's goin' to be plenty tough on you. Nobody out here has any use for a thief!"

The old cowhand saddled his horse and led the fiery animal out of the barn. Mack's gaze followed the nervous, wild-eyed mount with growing concern.

"You–you want me to ride behind the saddle on your horse?" he asked, as though not sure that would work at all.

Lefty frowned. "Now that's somethin' I've been studyin' out m'self. Old Buck ain't never been rode double, an' I don't figger he'd take too kindly to tryin' it now."

"Marie can ride double with me," DeeDee suggested, "and he can ride her horse."

The old man's eyes gleamed. "Now, that's a right smart idea. Get up there, young feller, an' be quick about it."

Numbly Mack mounted Marie's horse. Mama was trusting him to take care of her and the children. Now he had gotten himself caught and in an awful jam! And there wouldn't be anyone to look after the family.

DeeDee and Marie rode back to the Circle R ranch house with Lefty and their frightened young captive. Every now and then the girls glanced over at Mack. He was sitting stiffly in the saddle, fright twisting his dark, young features.

There was a question Marie wanted to ask him,

but they were almost home before she got up the courage to do so. At last she could wait no longer.

"Were you the one who was hiding in the mesquite near that old car when we stopped there the other day?"

Mack's face blanched. He grasped the saddle horn with his hand and pretended not to hear.

Marie repeated her question.

"No," He shot out the word. "I was not near the car when you went by on horseback." He caught his breath sharply. The instant he spoke he realized that he had said something he shouldn't have said. He had given himself away. Now they knew he had been there!

It was no use. He was getting in more trouble all the time. What would Mama think when she found out that she could no longer depend on him? The realization tore at his heart.

Marie turned in triumph to DeeDee. "There! That ought to prove to that brother of mine that I did see someone hiding by that old car."

DeeDee nodded. She knew how Marie felt to have proved that she was right, but she could not get elated about it. Not when Mack looked so dejected. It almost made her feel sorry that they had caught him.

When they finally reached the ranch house, Clarence and the boys were inside talking to Carmen. They heard the horses trot into the yard and came out.

"Hello there, Lefty," the rancher said. "I didn't expect to see you so soon."

"Neither'd I expect to be comin' over here to pay you a visit this week. But somethin' came up that I figured you ought to handle."

Clarence turned to eye Mack curiously.

"Who's this?"

Fear widened the boy's eyes, and his dark face went even whiter than it had been.

"This here's the thief the girls an' me captured." He gestured in Mack's direction. "This here's the character who's been stealin' my corn."

Before he was saved Clarence would have lost his temper and shouted angrily at the hapless boy before him. He had no more use for a thief than did any of his neighbors. And especially a Mexican thief. As far as he was concerned, they were much worse than any others. Now, however, his expression did not change and his voice was still even and well controlled.

"Suppose you get off the horse, son, and tell us what this is all about."

Mack did not answer him, but he dismounted and stood unsteadily before the tall rancher.

"Did you steal Lefty's corn?" Clarence asked him.

"Of course he stole my corn! We caught him goin' out of the barn with another sack. So you'd just as well save your breath askin' him anything. He'll only lie to you!"

But Clarence ignored Lefty. "How about it, son?"

Mack drew in a long breath. He wanted to protest his innocence, even though it meant lying once more. But that would do no good. This tall man would know whether or not he was telling the truth.

Carmen touched Clarence's arm lightly. "Let me talk to him," she said.

"In a little while. Right now there are some things I've got to find out." Then his stern face softened. "Let's take this young man into the house and talk to him."

Still terrified, Mack did as he was told. He didn't want to tell them about Mama and the little ones. On the long ride to the house, he had decided he would make them think he was alone so nothing bad would happen to the family. He determined to stick with that story even if he was put in jail.

But these people were not like anyone else he had ever known. They acted as though they really cared what happened to him. Under their gentle questioning he told them everything. He related how his papa had died in old Mexico and how hard it had been for the family to get the food and clothing they needed after that. He told them how Mama had said he must be the papa of the family and how they had come north in a desperate attempt to find her cousin.

"Everything would be all right if we find him," Mack assured them. "But the car broke down and we have no money. So I–I went out to get something to eat for Mama and the younger ones."

Lefty broke in finally. "Is that what you did with that corn you stole offa me?"

The boy nodded. "*Sí.* Mama ground it into meal with a stone and made tortillas. Only there are many of us and we don't have anything else to eat, so it takes much corn for tortillas."

Clarence leaned forward. "There's another thing I've got to find out about. Did you butcher a lamb a week or ten days ago?"

"*Sí,*" Mack said, smiling crookedly. "We had good meat when I killed the sheep, but Mama did not let me get any more." His voice raised. "But I decided that I had to get another when we get hungry, only I could not find any more."

Clarence wiped the moisture from his forehead. "What do your mother and the kids have to eat now?"

"I went out to get some more corn today," Mack said.

"You mean they have nothing to eat?" Carmen asked, horrified at the thought that the family would not have food.

"Mama saved some meal for tortillas for the little ones," he said.

"Where are they?" Carmen demanded. "We've got to go and get them."

"No!" Fear tightened Mack's voice. "No!"

"But we have to. We can't leave them out there with nothing to eat." She got to her feet. "Where are they, Mack? You must tell us!"

He didn't want to betray Mama and the little ones and take these people to them, but he could not do differently. He could not lie to them and make them believe it. Besides, there was something about these people that caused him to trust them.

At first Carmen thought she should stay at the ranch house and fix something for the hungry family to eat while Clarence went after them, but then she decided that she had better go along.

"If Mrs. Flores is like most of the women who come over from Mexico," she said, "she probably won't be able to speak English. She might be afraid to come with you. It's better that I go along so I can talk with her in her own language."

Clarence and Carmen took Mack with them to the highway bridge where the family had improvised a shelter. The rancher waited in the car while Carmen went with Mack to talk with his mother.

Mrs. Flores came out from under the bridge, worry clouding her careworn face. When she saw that her oldest son was back, she smiled broadly.

"What happened to you, Mack?" she asked in Spanish.

Before he could answer, Carmen began. She introduced herself and told her that she and her husband wanted to help.

At first Mrs. Flores did not understand. "We have hurt no one," she protested. "We only live here." She gestured with her hand. "We are hurting nothing."

Mrs. Flores was opposed to going to the ranch house. She protested that Mack would be able to look after them and that they would soon be able to continue their search for her cousin. When they found him, everything would be all right.

But Carmen would not be swayed. Gently she insisted that the Flores family go back to the ranch with her and Clarence.

At last Mrs. Flores called her children together and took them up to the highway where the car was standing. But she was apprehensive. To her it seemed that the end of everything had come.

"What will you do with us?" she asked fearfully.

"We'll fix you something to eat first," Carmen told her. "Then we'll fix a place for you to stay."

"But—"

Impulsively Carmen waved her protests aside.

Mrs. Flores got into the car reluctantly. Were they going to be held captive by these people? Would they never be able to continue their search for Cousin Hernandez?

In that moment she wished fervently that they had never left their village home in old Mexico. It would have been better to starve there among the people she knew and trusted than to fall into the hands of strangers.

Clarence drove them back to the ranch house. Carmen tried to talk with Mrs. Flores on the way, but the frightened woman sat erect, hands folded in her lap, her eyes glazed. This was something new and terrifying to her. The children sensed her fear, and it was mirrored in their black eyes. Nothing Carmen could do or say would erase any of it.

At the ranch Carmen guided the hungry, frightened family into the kitchen and had them sit down.

"I'll fix you something to eat," she said brightly, opening the refrigerator.

Mrs. Flores's eyes stared as she saw the food in the big white box. Never had she seen so much to eat in one place before, outside of a store.

"I'm sorry I don't have any cornmeal," Carmen went on, "so I can't make any tortillas. But we've got plenty of bacon and eggs."

Mack and his brothers and sisters had seen all the food, too. They looked at Mama, hopeful that she would let them eat. Mack knew what he was going to do if she said anything to him. He was going to tell her that he thought these must be good people, even though he still did not know what was going to happen to him for stealing the corn.

Carmen called them to the table after a short time and Mack put aside all thought about what they would do to him for stealing. He looked up at Carmen thankfully. Never had he seen so much food on the table at one time. And there was milk for little Carmelita. He thought his heart would burst with gratitude.

There wasn't room for the Flores family in the

house, so Clarence had the men clean out the second bunkhouse and fix it for the family. Mrs. Flores protested that they could not stay, that they wanted to go back to the improvised shelter they had made under the bridge.

"No," Clarence said firmly. He wasn't fluent in Spanish, but he could speak the language enough to make himself understood. "That's out of the question. You'll stay right here."

Mrs. Flores thought it all over from the time Mack was caught stealing the corn until now when the family was staying in the bunkhouse with plenty to eat for everyone. Never, even back in Mexico when Papa was alive, had they had such a nice place to live and so much to eat. Yet they had never seen these people before. She could not understand it. It worried her a little when she let herself ponder it. Maybe they would expect her to pay in money for the things they were doing for her and the children. Maybe they would make trouble for them when they found out she wasn't able to pay. She didn't have any pesos, let alone American dollars.

She got so frightened just thinking about what might happen that she felt they had to leave the Circle R right away. But Mack said that Mr. Roper would not let them leave.

"I talked to the man already, Mama," he told her. "He says we have to stay a while. He says he will tell us when we can go."

Concern gleamed in her black eyes. This was something new to worry about, something she had only vaguely considered before.

"Why do they not want us to go?" she asked.

Her oldest son shook his head. "He did not say, Mama. But it must not be money. He knows we do not have any. He only says he does not want us to go yet."

She said no more to her son about it. He had problems enough for one so young. But more than one night she lay awake thinking about this strange thing.

And the questions! That was something else that bothered her. Always they were asking questions, either the wife or that husband of hers. Questions about how they crossed the bridge to get into America from Mexico. And questions about who drove their old car all the way from Brownsville. And how they got so far without a license, whatever that was.

Mrs. Flores was not the only one who was disturbed about the situation, however. Clarence and Carmen Roper didn't understand everything either.

"I don't mind telling you, Carmen, I'm very much concerned," the rancher said. "Mrs. Flores is awfully vague when it comes to telling how she crossed the border with the children and how she got the necessary papers. You know, it isn't easy to get into this country if you're an alien, especially if you don't have any money."

Carmen was silent.

"She'd have to have money enough to get to her cousin, Hernandez, wherever he lives. And she'd have to have papers signed by him to show that he would be financially responsible for them."

"You don't suppose she came across without any papers, do you?"

"That's what I'm beginning to wonder. I want to keep them here until we can find out exactly what the situation is and see if we can help them."

Carmen went over to the window and looked out in the yard where the Flores children were playing.

"If she managed to get into the country without papers, she'd be in real trouble, wouldn't she?"

Clarence did not reply immediately.

"I don't know how serious the trouble would be," he said, "but if she doesn't have legal help, she would be taken back to Matamoros and dumped there. And she and the children wouldn't be any better off than they were before."

There was a long silence.

"I thought she would open up to you after you got acquainted with her, Carmen, but she's afraid to. I think you're going to have to tell her exactly what the situation is and why we've got to know the whole story."

"Do you think you'll be able to help them?" she asked.

"If I can get a lawyer on it now, I might."

The following morning Carmen went out to the

bunkhouse where the Flores family was living and invited Mrs. Flores in for coffee. Across the kitchen table Carmen explained the situation as best she could.

"My husband says he might be able to help you if you'll let us know exactly what the situation is. If he's going to help, he's got to know whether or not you've broken the law."

The Mexican woman reached a work-worn hand out slowly and touched her coffee cup.

"Is it against the law to do something so simple as to cross a bridge?" she asked.

"It isn't crossing the bridge. There are papers you are supposed to have that say it is all right for you to come to the United States."

The woman's hand was trembling as she sipped the coffee.

"I do not know about such things," she said. "I only know my little ones are hungry and my cousin Hernandez will help me feed them if we can get to him."

"I understand."

"What will they do to me?" Her voice broke.

Carmen shook her head. "I don't know, but my husband said he will get his attorney to see if he can get things straightened out."

The other woman thought about that. She didn't know what this attorney business was. The attorney fellow must be someone who could fix things right.

"But we have no money to pay."

Carmen laid a hand on her arm. "Don't worry about that. We'll take care of it."

Mrs. Flores shook her head in bewilderment. "Why do you do this?" she asked. "Why do you help us?"

Carmen replied quietly, "We do it because you need help and because we're–we're Christians." She would have said more, but Mrs. Flores seemed too distraught to think seriously about anything other than her problems.

For a long time after Mrs. Flores went back to the bunkhouse, she thought about the conversation she had just had with Carmen Roper. She had never known anyone so nice. And this being Christian. It was the first time she had ever heard anything like that.

She drew a deep breath. Just what had taken place she didn't know for sure. It was more Carmen's attitude than what she said. But in that conversation she came to see that she could trust this American woman and her husband.

* * *

The following morning Mack appeared at the door of the Ropers' ranch house den. Clarence was working on his books when the boy knocked timidly. At first Clarence didn't hear him and kept on working. Mack rapped again. At last Clarence realized that somebody was at the door. He looked up.

"Come on in."

Fearfully the Mexican boy did as he was bidden, eyeing the rancher suspiciously.

"I–" Mack fought for words. "I talked with Mama this morning. We think it is better to go now. We will not stay here anymore."

"Don't you like it here?" he asked.

"Oh, it is not that. It is not that at all. We are so many. It is better we go."

Clarence studied the boy's serious, young face.

"You haven't heard us complaining about how many of you there are, have you?"

Mack shook his head.

"We want you to stay here or we wouldn't have invited you."

This was even more difficult for Mack to understand than the fact that they had brought them to the ranch house in the first place.

"But–"

The rancher continued. "As a matter of fact, I planned on going out to talk with your mother this morning."

"*Sí?*"

"I just got in touch with my lawyer. He told me what to do so there would be no problems about your crossing the border. In fact, it looks as though everything is going to be straightened out. As soon as you have a job, the papers will all be signed."

Mack did not reply. This talk about lawyers,

whatever they were, and getting things straightened out sounded as though there could be bad trouble ahead for them. Trouble that this lawyer person might not be able to take care of. And what was this job Mr. Roper was talking about?

"It is better we go," Mack replied.

"You can't go. You don't have any money and your car isn't in shape to travel. Besides, you wouldn't be able to get past the next town, if you could get that far, without a license. It's a minor miracle to me that you were able to get up here from Brownsville without getting stopped." The rancher smiled reassuringly. "Trust me, Mack. My wife and I only want to help you."

The boy relaxed slightly. He had not known Mr. Roper long, but the Texan was a man of his word. That much was sure. Mack had seen men like that south of the Rio Grande. They looked a guy straight in the eye and told him what they thought. He might not like it, but he got the truth as they saw it. A man like Mr. Roper could be trusted.

"There's something else I'd like to talk over with you and your mother. We've been looking for someone to cook for the men who work for us. Do you think your mother would like to do that?"

"Cook?" He frowned. It wasn't that he didn't understand the word. Mr. Roper was offering his mother a job on the ranch, but it could not be true.

There had to be something wrong with such an offer. It was too wonderful. "Cook?" he repeated.

"Yes, we need a cook." Clarence took a deep breath. "We were talking about it last night. You and your mother and the kids could live in the bunkhouse."

There was a short silence.

"I'll furnish you with a place to live, all the meat you can eat, and cornmeal for tortillas. And I'll pay your mother a wage besides. How does that sound to you?"

Mack's eyes bulged. "It–it sounds *mucho–mucho–*" When he got excited his Spanish and English refused to separate. "It sounds *mucho* great!"

Mack scampered back to the bunkhouse where his mother was waiting for him.

"We will leave now?" Mama asked.

"Wait until I tell you!" Hurriedly he related what had happened.

"You not understand him, Mack." She spoke hesitantly. "Nobody would do such a nice thing for us. Nobody who has never seen us before would give us a place to live, cornmeal, meat, and money besides, just for cooking."

Mack was insistent. "But that is what he said! Two times I asked him and both times he told me the same thing. He said they would even fix up things with the–the lawyer so we will not get into trouble for crossing the bridge."

Thoughtfully Mrs. Flores turned the matter over

in her mind. For a relative one would do such a thing. But not for someone he never met before! Even in the stories they told around the campfires in their village back home, such things did not happen.

"Why do they do this, Mack?" she asked.

The lines in his face deepened. It was something for a person to ponder. They had strange talk about being Christian or whatever they called it. Maybe it had something to do with that. It was the only thing different about them from the other Americanos he had met. Yet, no one else would be so kind. It was something to lay carefully in the back of his mind and think on.

$* * *$

At last the day had come for the Davis triplets to leave the Circle R. The Roper family was going to the airport with them. They had gotten up an hour earlier than usual, had breakfast and their morning Bible readings, and Carmen and the girls finished the dishes. While that was going on, Clarence went into his den to do a bit of work.

A moment later Carmen came to the door. "Clarence," she said, "somebody just drove up."

He got to his feet and went to the window. "I haven't seen a car as big as that around here for quite a while."

"Neither have I," she said, laughing. "And pulling a horse trailer. That's quite a combination."

At that instant Phil burst in.

"Dad! You'll never believe it! Lefty Barrows just drove up!"

"What?"

"That's the truth. He's all dressed up and sitting in the back seat like he owns the whole shebang. He's even got a fellow driving it for him."

A moment later the old cowhand knocked at the door and Carmen went to answer it. Like Phil, she could scarcely believe what she saw. Lefty was dressed in a neat, hand-tailored business suit and was wearing a white, wide-brimmed hat. The easy, almost careless way in which he wore the clothes made it apparent that he was long used to them.

"Just wanted to stop by and thank you before I leave," he said.

He came into the house and sat down.

"You're sure leaving in style," Clarence said.

The old cowhand snorted. "Don't pay no attention to these here duds an' that car out there. That son of mine kept fussin' at me until I got both of them. I feel a lot more at home in a pair of blue jeans astride a salty little cow pony."

Clarence nodded. "Can't say that I blame you. But I let you stay in that old house because I figured you were broke and too proud to ask for help." There was a question in his voice that invited an explanation.

"I was worse off than broke. I was gettin' plumb suffocated living in that El Paso hotel. So as soon as my boy and his missus went to Europe, I got my driver to bring me and my favorite saddle horse out here where I was punchin' cows more'n forty years ago."

As the old ex-rancher talked, the Davis triplets crowded close, listening intently. They were sure going to have something to tell Danny and Kay when they got back to Fairview! It had been one of the most exciting summers of their lives.

THE DANNY ORLIS SERIES

The Danny Orlis series, by Bernard Palmer, delivers a blend of adventure, mystery, and suspense through various settings—from the Canadian wilderness to Guatemalan jungles. Danny Orlis, an adept outdoorsman, skilled athlete, and committed Christian, employs his quick thinking, calm bravery, and biblical solutions to confront everyday problems and hair-raising dangers. Early stories focus on Danny navigating school life, sports, and outdoor challenges, while in later books, Danny and his wife Kay provide wisdom and guidance to youngsters facing lifelike situations and challenges. Having sold over two million copies, this series has made Palmer a renowned author in Christian youth literature. Palmer is also the author of the Felicia Cartright series and various other series for Christian youth.

AVAILABLE FROM WWW.ANEKOPRESS.COM